A Treacherous Treasure

Mooseamuck Island Cozy Mystery Series
Book 3

Leighann Dobbs

Chapter 1

Dominic Benedetti shifted in his seat to avoid the glare of the early-morning sun in his eyes. Settling back in his chair, he focused his attention on the éclair on his plate. The din of the breakfast crowd inside Chowders receded to the background as he concentrated on neatly cutting the éclair in half, exposing the creamy center.

He speared a small piece with his fork, and his mouth watered with anticipation. The creamy custard and sweet dark chocolate blended on his tongue, conjuring up memories of his Italian roots in Boston's north end. He leaned back in the seat, a feeling of contentment washing over him.

Contentment wasn't something that Dom had ever expected to feel again. Not after his beloved wife Sophia had passed away a few years ago. Her death had nearly killed him, but her dying wish was for him to live a good life. And so he'd retired to Mooseamuck Island off the coast of Maine, a spot where he and Sophia had enjoyed many family vacations.

He'd been lonely at first, but he'd made friends quickly. They didn't get many folks who had "made the papers" on the island, and Dom had made them plenty as a consulting detective on high-profile cases down in Massachusetts. His fame had made him somewhat of a celebrity, and before he knew it, people were asking him to find lost keys and errant mittens ... not to mention murderers.

He'd even been accepted into the group of islanders that breakfasted at Chowders every morning. And he'd managed to talk the restaurant owner, Sarah, into adding some Italian dishes to the menu. Naturally, he'd volunteered to taste test each and every one of them.

"How's the éclair, Dom?" Sarah passed by the table, her long blond ponytail sliding over her shoulder as she glanced down at his plate.

Dom pinched his fingers at the corner of his mouth then flung them apart as he said, "Delizioso!"

The praise earned a smile from Sarah that warmed Dom's heart. Dom thought of Sarah as a surrogate daughter, and he was glad to see there was no trace of the hint of sadness that had previously dimmed her smile.

He figured the new happiness was due mostly to the young man, Shane McDonough, whose shoulder her hand now lingered on as she passed his table on her way to the kitchen. But Dom also thought that maybe he could take a little bit of credit for Sarah's uplifted demeanor.

If it hadn't been for his help in solving a murder case the past summer, Sarah's secret would never have been revealed, and she would not have been free to enjoy life without her past dragging her down. Of course, Dom couldn't take all the credit for that. Some of that belonged to Claire Watkins, a former colleague he'd been surprised to discover also lived on the island.

Back in his consulting days, Dom and Claire had worked several cases together. While the cases had been solved successfully, Dom wouldn't exactly say that he enjoyed working with Claire. He had a much different approach to investigating than she did and, though he had a grudging respect for her methods, he usually preferred to work alone.

Sure, he had to admit that the last case they'd solved, right here on the island, had been fun. He'd enjoyed seeing her apply her feel-good method of ferreting out people's motives while he used his strictly logical go-by-the-book method of analyzing the clues.

The truth was, the two murder cases that had happened on the island since Dom had moved here had added excitement and zest to his life. Claire, not so much. And though Dom didn't want harm to come to any of his friends or neighbors, he had to admit that he would dearly love to keep his skills sharp by investigating another murder, even if it meant partnering with Claire Watkins.

Speaking of which, where was Claire?

Dom frowned at the empty seat on the other side of the Formica table. It wasn't like Claire to be late.

Thwack!

"Isn't that right, Dom?"

Dom jumped at the sound of the cane hitting the table and turned to see Norma Hopper, the island's resident artist and crotchety old lady, looking at him quizzically.

"Isn't what right?" Dom asked.

Norma jerked her head toward the window. "We don't need a fancy-schmancy pharmacy."

Dom glanced across the road, where a backhoe was getting ready to break ground for the new pharmacy. The pharmacy had been a bone of contention on the island for several months. Some of the islanders hated the idea of a big, boxy concrete building, thinking it would ruin the quaint charm of the island. Others liked the convenience of being able to get their prescriptions here instead of going to the mainland for those the local small-time pharmacy did not carry.

"I don't know," Dom said. "It would be a lot more convenient."

"Pfftt. We can get anything we want at McDougal's. We don't need a big boxy goliath to ruin the look of the island," Norma persisted.

Next to Norma, Tom Landry nodded his head. "I agree, Norma. I don't like the way this town is changing. It's becoming more like the mainland every day."

"That's right," Mae Bidderford chimed in. "Pretty soon there'll be a strip mall and drive-thrus on every corner."

Tom clucked and patted her hand. "Let's hope that doesn't happen."

Mae's cheeks flushed, and her eyes sparked. The two octogenarians had grown up on the island. Their families had been engaged in a feud since Tom and Mae were in kindergarten, and the two of them had always disagreed just to spite each other. The corners of Dom's lips ticked up as he noted they were in agreement on this subject. In fact, they had been in agreement on practically everything since they'd discovered their true feelings for one another the previous summer.

"I don't know, I think it could be convenient, too. McDougal doesn't carry everything, and a lot of us have to ferry to the mainland for medicine."

Jane Kuhn, the island's postmistress, spoke up from the end of the table.

"Yeah, it can be a pain," Alice James said without looking up from her knitting. The needles clacked together with a metallic beat as she stitched the fuzzy purple yarn. Alice was always knitting something ... most of which she traded or gave as unwanted gifts. Dom hoped the purple scarf—or whatever it was—was not slated for him.

"Well, Benjamin Hill doesn't think it will be convenient." Mae squinted at the window, and Dom followed her gaze.

Outside, the rusty yellow shovel of the bulldozer hung poised in the air, waiting to bite down into the earth. Clyde Hubbel sat in the driver's seat, a splash of red from his flannel shirt visible through the dirty glass. In front of the backhoe, an elderly man—Benjamin Hill— gestured wildly. Beside him, his grandson, Allen, made futile attempts to calm him. A handful of islanders stood around in a circle sipping steaming coffee from Styrofoam mugs, watching the show.

"That's no surprise. Benjamin protests everything," Jane said.

"Uh oh, here comes Matheson. He'll probably kick Benjamin out," Tom said.

A white pickup truck driven by the owner of the land, Jacob Matheson, pulled onto the lot. Dom's right brow twitched as he watched the man get out and stomp toward Benjamin. His finger flew up to the bushy brow, patting it down. Must have just been an itch, Dom thought. His famous eyebrow tingles usually signified some sort of mystery or clue was present, and there was no mystery here.

"I'll lay right down and you'll have to dig through me." Benjamin's voice—unusually strong for such an old man—could be heard clearly from across the street.

"He should give it up. It's a lost cause," Hiram Moody said from the corner table, his spoon poised halfway to his mouth.

"Yeah, looks like Jacob's not going to stop," someone else added as the backhoe started up.

Dom looked out again. Benjamin's gesturing was becoming more animated as he paced behind Jacob. Allen followed them, apparently trying to calm his grandfather down.

"You know, I heard that might be one of the sites where Captain Kidd buried his treasure," Alice said, her needles still clacking.

Dom swiveled his attention in her direction. "Really? Has there been pirate treasure found on the island?"

"No, but it's a known fact he buried treasure in Maine. Why, some of it's been found in Portland, in Biddeford, and on Richmond Island."

"That's right." Mae nodded then leaned into the table and lowered her voice. "Rumor has it that Mooseamuck Island was where he stashed most of his booty, though."

"You don't say." Dom's eyebrow twitched again as he turned back to the scene going on outside the window. More onlookers had arrived outside, and by now most everyone in the diner had one eye on their breakfast and the other on the lot across the street. Even Alice's knitting needles had stopped clacking.

Out of the corner of his eye, Dom saw Claire's little brown Fiat. Though she pulled it into the Chowders parking lot, her attention was riveted on the backhoe. Dom figured she wouldn't be able to resist getting into the middle of whatever was going on over there. She'd want to use her human behavior skills to try to analyze Benjamin's motivations and attempt to smooth out the situation. Good luck to her. Benjamin was becoming more distraught as the backhoe inched forward to a spot Jacob Matheson indicated.

Claire got out of her car.

The backhoe stopped on the spot, its gears grinding as Clyde readied the shovel.

Dom's eyebrow twitched again.

Benjamin Hill ran in front of the shovel, his cane held high, his voice threatening. "Stop! I'm warning you, if you dig here, you'll be sorry!"

***

Claire Watkins stood beside her Fiat and stretched, breathing in the sharp saltiness of the crisp ocean air. She snugged her lightweight canvas jacket around her. It was early spring, and the morning still had a chill.

The sound of heavy machinery distracted her, and she looked across the street to see a small crowd watching Benjamin Hill wave his cane in the air as he gestured wildly in front of the backhoe.

Ahh yes, today was the groundbreaking for the new pharmacy, Claire remembered.

Benjamin was causing quite a ruckus, and she couldn't say she blamed him. A longtime island resident, he was in his early nineties and one of the islanders who had been most vocal about his opinions on new construction. Like many of the old-timers, Benjamin resisted change.

All of the island residents, no matter what their age, were careful about new development, though. The island drew thousands of tourists in the summer and, since many of the businesses relied on tourist dollars to survive, no one wanted to ruin its quaint, old-fashioned look.

But some things were necessities. The current pharmacy had been built in the 1950s and run by two generations of the McDougal family. It didn't have the facilities to carry all of the medicines that the island residents, and sometimes the tourists, needed. After many heated arguments, a new pharmacy was approved, and today construction had begun.

Claire let out a sigh. She supposed the new pharmacy was progress, but like Benjamin, she hated to see the landscape of the island she'd grown up on changing.

The smell of bacon made her stomach grumble, and her eyes drifted over to Chowders, where she could see the regulars she breakfasted with sitting at the table by the window. She hadn't eaten yet, only taken her medicinal tea of apple cider vinegar and lemon in warm water—part of her strict natural health regimen.

Claire considered herself fortunate to enjoy amazingly good health for a woman in her seventies. She was spry, slim, and, most importantly, still had all her wits about her. But the medicinal tea, however healthy it was, was no substitute for a good breakfast of oatmeal or poached eggs, and Claire was hungry.

She'd just started toward the restaurant when another shout from Benjamin Hill caught her attention.

"Stop! I'm warning you, if you dig here, you'll be sorry!"

My, he was being overly dramatic. Claire had known there would be some opposition to the groundbreaking, but she hadn't expected Benjamin to be so passionate about it.

Claire's attention hovered between her breakfast waiting inside Chowders and checking out the ruckus across the street.

"Listen, Benjamin, you have no right to obstruct construction. I could have you arrested." Jacob Matheson, his fists clenched at his sides, faced Benjamin, only about six inches of space between them.

"Arrested! Don't threaten me, young man." Benjamin's voice sounded nearly hysterical.

Claire's stomach nagged her. She glanced back at Chowders.

Breakfast or ruckus?

"Move it, old man."

The harsh words had Claire swiveling her head back toward the ruckus. Jacob was right up in Benjamin's face, which was turning a shade of red deep enough to have Claire's heart twisting in concern. Benjamin was not a young man, and all this commotion couldn't be good for him. Benjamin's grandson, Allen, fluttered around trying to defuse the situation, but his attempts were largely ignored.

Claire sighed and reluctantly turned away from Chowders. Someone had to go over there and calm Benjamin down, and with her skills as a psychologist, she was well suited to do it. She wouldn't be able to forgive herself if something happened to Benjamin and she didn't do anything to stop him from getting even more worked up.

The onlookers spread apart to make room as Claire approached the group.

"Hey, Benjamin, what's going on?" she asked, hoping her matter-of-fact tone would distract him from his anger.

"This young whippersnapper here means to dig up the site! Why, it's a historical landmark. We can't let him do that, Claire," Benjamin pleaded.

Jacob stepped back from Benjamin, resting his hands on his hips. "That's where you're wrong. I have the permits from the town to build here. Therefore this is not an officially recognized historical site. I'm here legally, and you are obstructing."

"Legal schmegel. Don't you have any respect for island history?"

Claire ventured forward and put a soothing hand on Benjamin's arm. "Come on, Benjamin, those rumors about pirate treasure buried here are just that—rumors."

"T'aint no truth to them. Else if there was, you'd a seen them burying it with yer own eyes. Weren't you around three hundred years ago?" Chester O'Grady teased from the crowd. Chester and Benjamin were friends, about the same age, and Claire knew the teasing was done with good intentions. It was likely that Chester wanted to calm Benjamin down as well.

The crowd laughed, and Claire was relieved to see that the joke did soothe Benjamin somewhat.

He shot Jacob an angry glare. "You mainlanders are ruining the island."

"Now Benjamin, you know we had much debate about this, and we voted. The majority of the people wanted this pharmacy," Claire soothed.

"That's right, Grandfather. Now relax. This isn't good for you." Allen tried to put his arms around the old man's shoulders, but Benjamin shook him off.

"I know what's good for me and what isn't. And what isn't is this young galoot digging up this site!" Benjamin gestured violently at Jacob with his cane but reluctantly let Allen lead him away from the backhoe.

14

Jacob nodded to Clyde, and the backhoe revved up, the shovel rising high in the air, its claw opening as it descended toward the earth.

The show now over, the crowd started to disperse as the backhoe bit into the earth, eating up scoops of dirt and depositing them in a pile.

"Come on now, Benjamin, I'll buy you breakfast." Claire tugged him toward Chowders.

The old man resisted stubbornly. "I don't want breakfast. We need to stop them."

Allen looked ruefully at the backhoe as it took another bite. "It's a lost cause, I'm afrai—"

Thunk.

Claire stopped in her tracks.

"That didn't sound good," Allen echoed her thoughts.

They turned to see the construction workers peering into the hole.

"I knew it!" Benjamin broke free and started back to the site, where the workers were now pointing excitedly.

The other onlookers had rushed back, and a crowd now ringed the hole. One of the workers had jumped down inside and was shoveling dirt out by hand. Claire pushed her way to the front, vaguely aware of people rushing over from Chowders adding to the growing crowd.

Inside the hole, a worker brushed dirt off a large honey-colored oak box. It was rectangular, about two feet by three feet, and encrusted with centuries of dirt. The oversized, curly black iron hinges were dark with rust, and there was a thin edging around the box that glinted like gold in the sunlight.

"Well, will ya fancy that," Chester said. "There really is a dang pirate treasure buried here."

The crowd erupted in whispered speculation, everyone wondering what would be in the chest. Golden doubloons? Gemstones? Silver? The men dug carefully around the box to expose the latch, from which a broken iron lock dangled.

One of the workmen grasped the edge of the lid then looked up at Jacob. "Should we open it?"

Jacob pursed his lips in thought as the crowd chimed in.

"Yes."

"Of course."

"Open the dang thing."

"Okay." Jacob nodded. "Open it up, but whatever is in there belongs to me."

"Or the historical society," someone muttered.

The workman slowly pushed up on the lid so it was open just a crack. The crowd held its breath as the hinges creaked, and the box groaned as if

16

angry over being disturbed after so many years in the ground.

Claire noticed that her breakfast gang had made their way to the front row, with Norma standing beside her.

Everyone leaned closer to get the first glimpse of the treasure inside. Norma's cane, with its ivory handle in the shape of a bulldog's head, rested precariously on the edge of the hole as she craned her wrinkled neck to see into the hole.

The man raised the lid halfway, and Norma gasped, then turned away disgusted. "Well, ain't that a kick in the pants. There's no treasure in there. It's just a pile of old pirate bones."

Chapter 2

"Pirate bones?"

Claire recognized the voice of Dominic Benedetti as he pushed his way to the front of the crowd, circling the hole to look at the scene from all angles.

Probably looking for clues, Claire surmised. As she watched him, she noticed his finger snake up and pat his bushy eyebrow—a behavior she'd noticed many times while they were on a case. Usually it signified a clue or lead, but that couldn't be the case here.

What could there possibly be of investigatory interest in a pirate skeleton that was over three hundred years old?

Memories of her career as a criminal psychologist in Massachusetts surfaced, and a smile tugged at her lips. She'd loved investigating crimes. The thrill of the chase. The satisfaction of putting a killer behind bars. The only fly in the ointment of her long and illustrious career had been Dominic Benedetti, with whom she'd been teamed on more cases than she cared to remember.

Dom was a highly skilled and successful investigator, but Claire couldn't really say that she'd enjoyed working with him. Oh, they'd solved a good many cases together, but his insistence on only using physical evidence to form their theories drove her crazy. Claire had proven over and over again that her methods of getting inside the suspects' heads and studying their body language and facial expressions to figure out who the killer was and why they killed worked. Dom never seemed to want to admit that, though, and so their working relationship down south had been a bit rocky.

She was surprised to discover that he'd moved to Mooseamuck Island and saddened that his wife had died. She, herself, had been away from the island for most of her adult life, returning only a few years ago to care for her dying father. She vaguely remembered Dom mentioning vacations here during their time working together, but she'd never dreamed he'd end up living here.

She had to admit, she'd been a bit annoyed at first. Oh, she liked him well enough as a person but didn't necessarily want him to be her neighbor. But then, the two murder cases they'd solved on the island had softened her toward him.

He seemed gentler now, as if grief had mellowed him and made him more accepting of her ways.

She frowned as she watched him angling his head this way and that. A light sparked in his eyes as if he was about to embark on catching a real killer. But with a three-hundred-year-old victim, the killer would be long dead. That took all the fun out of it for Claire, but maybe Dom was bored and needed another investigation, even if it wouldn't bring anyone to justice.

She could sympathize. She never felt more alive than when she was running down clues and chasing bad guys. The truth be told, she wouldn't mind investigating another murder right now, too. But not a three-hundred-year-old one. There would be no living suspects to sharpen her psychological skills on.

Still, if Dom saw something that might be of interest ...

She angled her head to inspect the trunk. The side of the trunk was taller than the front, and from her position, she could only see a skeletal hand sticking up over the edge. She assumed the rest of the skeleton was inside. Maybe she should make her way to the front where Dom was and find out for sure.

"I guess this will hold up the building of the pharmacy." Claire turned to see Jane Kuhn, her best friend since kindergarten.

"Oh, hi, Jane. I hadn't thought about it, but I suppose you're right." Claire and Jane elbowed their way around the hole, trying to get to the front where Dom was. Claire's suspicious mind immediately wondered if someone had planted the chest there to delay the pharmacy, but then she realized how ridiculous that was. Where would someone get an old trunk with a skeleton in it? And besides, the ground had been undisturbed —it would have been obvious if someone had recently dug here.

As they reached Dom, a spark of sun glinted off Jane's necklace, and Claire frowned at her friend. She was sure she knew all of Jane's jewelry pieces, and this necklace was not one of them. It looked new. And expensive. Claire's eyes drifted over to Jane's shiny new Volvo parked in the Chowders parking lot. Jane certainly had a lot of extra money to spend lately. Odd, because Claire knew that Jane was typically worried about money, since her job as postmistress did not pay a lot.

But it seemed Jane had quite a few secrets from Claire lately, not the least of which was some sort of relationship she was apparently having with the detective from the mainland, Frank Zambuco. Had Zambuco bought her the necklace? Claire's nose wrinkled at the thought. Zambuco was not one of her favorite people. He was obnoxious, abrasive, and overbearing. The thought of him and Jane together made her stomach churn. Good thing she hadn't just chowed down a big breakfast.

As if reading her thoughts, one of the construction workers said, "I guess we better call Robby. He'll probably have to call in that detective from the mainland."

Jane's face took on a pinched look, her body stiffened, her eyes taking on a faraway look.

"Are you all right?" Claire focused her attention on Jane.

Jane's brow creased, then her eyes cleared, and she waved her hand dismissively. "Fine. I ... just realized that I forgot to pay the check at the diner. I treated today."

And with that, Jane turned and disappeared through the crowd.

Claire stared after her friend. That seemed like oddly exaggerated behavior for forgetting to pay a restaurant check. Claire thought it might be more than that. Maybe it was the mention of Zambuco's name ... or maybe the sight of the skeleton. Because of her former career, Claire was used to dead bodies, but Jane wasn't. She imagined the sight of a skeleton—even a three-hundred-year-old one—could be disturbing.

The breakfast regulars had appeared beside Claire, Tom and Mae standing very close together, Alice with two stainless steel knitting needles sticking out of a skein of purple yarn at the top of her bag, and Norma wearing her hat with the wide brim that Claire suspected was more for keeping people out of the cantankerous old woman's space than for protection from the sun.

Claire glanced at the rest of the crowd to see a variety of looks on their faces, ranging from disgust to interest, before turning her attention to look into the box herself.

From her new position, she had a clear view of the full contents of the chest for the first time. The skeleton looked to be still intact, its legs drawn up to its chest as if it had been folded to fit, which it must have. Surprisingly, the old oak boards of the chest had held together all these years.

Norma gestured toward the chest with her cane. "Well, how do you suppose a pirate got in there? Fell in by accident?"

Claire continued her inspection of the contents. Even though the chest was intact, it must not have been airtight; otherwise there would have been a mummy in there instead of a skeleton. Claire could see the remnants of black pants and a blue plaid flannel shirt. Then her breath caught in her throat as she saw the dark stain on the bottom of the trunk and the dagger lying on top of it.

Dom's answer to Norma confirmed her sudden realization. His finger came up to smooth his brow, his eyes still fixed on the chest as he said, "A pirate did not fall in here by accident. This was murder."

***

Dom was still busy with his visual assessment of the crime scene when Robby Skinner, current chief of police and Claire's nephew, pulled up in his car. Dom prided himself on noticing abnormalities and locking in on potential clues in modern crime scenes and was pleased to find that he had those skills with centuries-old scenes, too.

He noticed the lock on the chest, while hanging open, seemed to be newer than the apparently three-hundred-year-old pirate chest. He also noticed the remnants of flannel shirt. Dom was pretty sure pirates didn't wear flannel. No, this was no pirate murder. This was more contemporary. But when?

Dom knew nothing of skeletons. He didn't know how to determine how long the body had been buried. Ten years? Thirty years? One hundred years? He had no idea. He made a mental note to call one of his old associates who had expertise in this area.

"Okay, clear on out." Robby elbowed his way through the crowd, which parted reluctantly to let him up to the front. He glanced at Dom and then Claire.

"Dom. Auntie. Fancy seeing you two at a crime scene." Robby looked into the hole, his face screwing up. "What is going on here?"

"Well, as you can see, we dug up a treasure chest with a skeleton in it," Norma cut in from the crowd, which Robby's two deputies were now trying to push back.

Robby looked around at the backhoe. Jacob stood next to it with his hands on his hips. The workmen lined up next to him, watching.

"And just how did this happen?" Robby asked.

"It's the groundbreaking for the new pharmacy," Claire said.

"I know that," Robby said with an exasperated sigh. "How did this treasure chest get here?"

Claire shrugged. "They dug it up. Apparently it's been buried here for hundreds of years."

"I told you you'd be sorry!" Benjamin Hill yelled out from the middle of the crowd.

Jacob turned his scowling face in Benjamin's direction then stomped over to Robby. "Look, this thing is hundreds of years old. It's got nothing to do with my project, so I hope you aren't going to stop construction because of this old skeleton."

Robby rubbed his hand across his face. "Truth is, I'm not sure what to do. Was there a crime? How would we even investigate it? Everyone involved is likely long dead. But I do have to stop digging for now. I already put in a call to the mainland, and we'll have to wait and see what they say about it."

Jacob threw his hands up in the air. "I didn't think this day could get any worse. You realize this is costing me a lot of money, don't you?"

"Sorry, Jacob. There's not much I can do about it." Robby turned to the crowd. "Okay, everybody, go home. There's nothing more to see here."

"Robby, I don't think—"

Dominic was interrupted by Robby. "That includes you." Robby turned to Claire. "And you, Auntie Claire. I can't very well let you guys hang around crime scenes when I make everyone else leave. I can't play favorites, or no one in town will listen to me."

Dom shrugged. He had been about to tell Robby his observations, but if the young man didn't want to listen ... Dom glanced over at

Chowders to see most everyone had retreated to the restaurant and were angling for position by the large picture window.

Dom heard the whistle that indicated the ferry was pulling in. That meant Zambuco would be coming shortly. Dom had no desire to match wits with the aggravating detective.

He raised a brow at Claire and tilted his head toward Chowders. Claire nodded, and they started in that direction. In front of them, Allen Hill escorted Benjamin to their shiny black Cadillac coupe, opening the passenger door and waiting for his grandfather to step in. As they passed them, Dom heard Benjamin say, "This is all going to end badly, boy, I tell you. Should've left well enough alone."

They were just getting settled at their table inside Chowders when Zambuco pulled up. Dom, a fastidious dresser himself who prided himself on staying in good shape, noticed that Zambuco did not appear as slovenly as usual. Not that he was dressing any better, but at least he didn't have stains on his shirt today.

Chowders was abuzz with talk of pirates, treasure, and murder. Sarah hustled orders out from behind the counter. Claire ate her bowl of oatmeal as they watched out the window.

"Looks like we dodged a bullet there." Claire nodded toward Zambuco. In the previous two island murders, Zambuco had taken a dim view of finding Claire and Dom at the crime scene. He didn't like the retired detectives butting in on his cases.

"Zambuco can't really fault you for being here on the scene. Half the town was here. Besides, he only gets upset when you guys are going to investigate, and there is nothing to investigate ... is there?" Tom Landry asked.

"Right. Who cares about an old pirate that died hundreds of years ago?" Alice crossed the yarn over her needle then pulled it down through the previous stitch.

Dom pressed his lips together and looked out the window. "That's the thing. The person in that trunk may not have died hundreds of years ago."

Mae sucked in a breath. "What do you mean?"

Dom saw a knowing look in Claire's eye. So she had caught on to the fact that the flannel shirt was more modern. Dom felt a swell of pride. He'd been trying to teach Claire how to be more observant about the physical evidence, and it looked like maybe his teachings were finally starting to work. Perhaps it would not be so disagreeable to work with her on another case after all.

"I can't really say too much," Dom answered Mae's question. "Not until the police have a look at it."

Across the street, the police removed the skeleton carefully from the chest and laid it on a stretcher. As they did, something fell from the body. Dom's brow began to tingle. He squinted, practically pressing his face against the glass to see what it was—a metal buckle from a pair of suspenders. That definitely had not existed in the sixteen hundreds.

Zambuco held up his hand to stop them. He bent to look at the buckle then gestured for one of his minions to bag it as evidence.

Once the skeleton and chest were loaded into the ambulance, there was not much to watch. Everyone who had been clustered around the window now retreated to their tables.

"Well, that's that. I guess the show is over." Chester pulled his wallet out of his back pocket, peeled out some bills, and tossed them onto the table. Most of the other patrons did the same.

Mae scooted her chair closer to Dom. "What do you mean, the person didn't die three hundred years ago? And if not, then how did he get buried in a pirate chest and who put him there?"

Chapter 3

Claire sat on the stone bench in her garden, drinking in the bird's-eye view of the sapphire-blue Atlantic Ocean. The large garden was Claire's pride and joy, a respite from the stresses of everyday life. Located on the east side of the stone cottage that had been her childhood home, it offered spectacular sunrise views from its vantage point three quarters of the way up on Israel Head Hill.

Her mother had designed the garden, carefully mapping out the layout and planting the flowers. Her father had built planters, installed the stone benches, and made the sturdy fence at the east edge of the yard that kept one from falling down the steep cliff onto the scenic road that wound around directly below. Her mother had died decades ago, and the garden had fallen into disrepair in Claire's father's later years. Claire had spent the last two years restoring it after having cared for her father in his final year.

Early-spring greenery sprouted from the shrubs and flowers. The daffodils and tulips had already bloomed. The thought of the garden poised to come to life with colorful flowers and lush leaves lifted Claire's spirits.

She was too far up the hill to hear the soothing sounds of the ocean, but she could hear the seagulls calling and smell the salty sea air. It was just past noon, and the sun was at its strongest. It warmed her shoulders, soothing and relaxing her.

But even in her beloved garden with the soothing sun and tranquil view, something picked at Claire. She was still disturbed about the grim discovery earlier that morning. Not because of the sight of a skeleton; that didn't bother her at all. What did bother her was that she suspected the murder was more recent than three hundred years. Much more recent. Which meant one of the islanders may have been involved.

Claire did not feel confident about Zambuco investigating it, either. He was an outsider who did not have the interests of the islanders at heart. Well, except maybe Jane.

In any event, she couldn't very well let him take control of the case and pin it on an islander just to satisfy his higher-ups with quick closure. The happenings on Mooseamuck Island didn't seem to be as important to the mainland police, and she was afraid they'd be too hasty in their eagerness to close the case swiftly. They'd done that before and almost incarcerated the wrong person—one of her dearest friends. She wasn't about to let something like that happen again.

"Meow!"

Claire looked down to see the fluffy Maine Coon cat she called Porch Cat winding around her azalea bush.

"Hey, Porch Cat." Claire greeted the cat by extending her fingers, and the animal came over to sniff. Probably looking for one of the treats that Claire often left out for the wandering cat. Though Porch Cat had a home, she preferred to spend her days meandering around the island, visiting various homes and businesses. Claire didn't know if the cat got a treat at every house, but Claire usually tried to provide something at hers. But Claire had been too deep in thought to think about putting anything out for the cat this afternoon.

"Sorry, buddy, I don't have anything."

Porch Cat gazed up at her with brilliant green eyes.

"Meow." She trotted over to a mound of peonies and started digging, looking up at Claire expectantly as if trying to convey some sort of message.

"Digging. Yes I need to be digging into this case, I know."

"Mew." Porch Cat stopped digging and trotted over to rub her cheek against Claire's leg as if rewarding the human for getting the message.

"Unfortunately, this case is very old. A cold case," Claire said to the cat. "And solving it will depend a lot on the physical evidence. That's not my forte."

"Meow!" Porch Cat caught Claire's eye and then jerked her head up, toward the top of Israel Head Hill. Claire followed her gaze. A condo development had gone in near the top of the hill several years ago, much to the protest of the islanders. From Claire's spot at the edge of her garden, she could just see the edge of one of the patios. Dom's patio, to be exact.

"Oh I see, you think I should team up with him."

"Meow." Porch Cat flicked her bushy black-and-brown-striped tail. Then, her visit apparently over, she trotted away, disappearing inside the thick growth of ornamental grasses at the edge of the garden.

Claire settled back on the bench. Perhaps it wasn't such a bad idea to enlist Dom's aid. But how? She didn't want to go begging him to work with her. No, that would not do. Something more subtle ...

Claire's eyes slid over to her kitchen window. She'd just baked some healthy coconut-flour-and-cacao brownies. She knew how much Dom liked his desserts. Wouldn't it be neighborly to bring him some?

Her mind made up, Claire pushed up off the bench. In the kitchen, she quickly arranged the brownies on a clear crystal plate and started up the hill toward Dom's. It was a steep climb, but that didn't bother her. She often walked it as part of her health regimen.

She reached Dom's door and hesitated. Though they spent many hours working together and socializing with the regulars, she had only been to his place a few times. She suddenly felt awkward at visiting unannounced.

The door jerked open, surprising Claire. Dom stood in the threshold, his eyes wide with surprise.

"Claire. What are you doing here? I saw someone come up the walk, and when they didn't knock ..."

Claire held up the plate of brownies. "Sorry, I had my hands full with this plate. I made these fresh and thought you might want to try them."

Dom looked at the plate suspiciously. "What are they?"

Claire cleared her throat. "They're coconut flour, butter, eggs, cacao, vanilla, and maple syrup. Very healthy and delicious. You know you shouldn't be eating all those sugary and fat-laden Italian treats all the time."

Dom's left brow ticked up. "Well, I didn't realize you were so concerned about my health." He stepped aside and opened the door. "Do come in."

Dom's place was neat as a pin, everything perfectly centered and placed where it should be. Claire remembered Dom's penchant for having things exactly in their place and lined up precisely. Some sort of obsessive-compulsive disorder, she presumed, though she'd never actually say that to Dom. She followed him to the small but well-apportioned kitchen, where he took out two china plates and perfectly centered a brownie on each.

"Coffee?" Dom asked.

"I'd love some." Claire took the plates to the table and waited while Dom poured coffee. Next to the sliding glass door that led to the patio, Dom's parakeets chirped in their cage. Claire smiled at the colorful birds. Romeo and Juliet. The male, in vibrant shades of green and yellow, clung to the side of the cage, watching them with intelligent black eyes. The female, in soft aqua and white, sat on the perch preening. "I see your birds are enjoying the spring view."

"Yes, they love looking out at the ocean." Dom took a tentative bite of the brownie, his face registering a parade of emotions as he swirled it around in his mouth like he was tasting a glass of expensive wine.

"This is surprisingly good," he admitted. "But I'm not giving up my cannolis or éclairs just yet."

An uncomfortable silence descended on them as they sipped their coffee. Dom's body language told Claire that he wanted to ask her something but was hesitant. Hopefully it was something about investigating the pirate skeleton.

"Tweemup. Intwestwigate," Romeo chirped.

Claire turned toward the cage to find Romeo staring at her. Did he just say to team up and investigate?

Claire turned back toward Dom to find him also looking at the bird.

"About that skeleton ..." They said the words at the same time.

Dom chuckled. "As you have already deduced, the victim was not a pirate."

Claire nodded. "Indeed. He, or she, wasn't put in there three hundred years ago, but when do you think he was?"

"I'm no expert on skeletal remains, so I'm not sure," Dom looked over the rim of his cup at Claire. "I did make a call to an old colleague, and he said it takes forty or fifty years for the bones to become brittle, but I couldn't tell if those bones were brittle or not."

"So we have no idea when the murder occurred."

"Not necessarily. I can narrow it down somewhat." Dom put his cup on the table and leaned forward. "Perhaps you noticed the remnants of the victim's shirt?"

Claire nodded. "The blue flannel. That's how I knew it wasn't a pirate."

"Right. Well, flannel shirts weren't invented until the late 1800s. Furthermore, I saw a suspender buckle fall from the body when the police moved it. Again, those were not invented until the late 1800s."

Claire pressed her lips together. "So the murder could have happened as long as a hundred years ago."

"Or as close as ten years ago."

"You don't think it was that close, do you?"

"Hard to tell."

"If it was, then the murderer could still be among us."

"Indeed."

Claire pressed her lips together. This was exactly what she was afraid of. "And if the police start an investigation ... well, you know what can happen with Zambuco. He's liable to incarcerate the wrong person!"

Dom nodded. "But if it was a long time ago, there may not even be any suspects that are still alive."

"It would be helpful to know just when the murder occurred."

"Or who the victim was."

A moment of silence passed between them.

"I'm sure the police will figure that out pretty quickly," Claire said. "They probably already have, but I doubt Zambuco would share with us."

"Zambuco wouldn't ... but maybe Robby would," Dom suggested.

Claire hated to try to wrangle police information out of her nephew. She knew he could get into trouble—maybe even lose his job—if anyone found out, so she only used her powers of persuasion on him when it was absolutely necessary.

"The murder is decades old. It might not even be worth investigating. It's likely no one left living on the island even remembers anything about it." Claire remembered how desperate Benjamin Hill had seemed at the groundbreaking. He'd claimed he didn't want to ruin a historical site, but was that really why he didn't want them to dig there?

"But if it isn't that old, do you really trust Zambuco to get it right?" Dom asked.

"No."

Dom polished off the last of his second brownie and looked up with a twinkle of excitement in his eye. "Then I guess it's up to us to figure it out."

***

A pang of guilt shot through Claire as she stood on the doorstep of Robby's modest house. She hated coming to Robby on the pretext of bringing dessert so that she could pump him for information. Reminding herself that gaining this information might save one of the islanders from being unjustly accused, she shuffled the plate from her right hand to her left, raised her fist, and knocked.

A few seconds later, she heard shuffling noises from behind the door, and then it opened, revealing her nephew's smiling face. His obviously genuine pleasure at seeing her and his lack of suspicion at her ulterior motives produced another pang of guilt.

Robby's eyes drifted from hers to the plate, stacked high with the gooey brownies. "Auntie, you brought brownies!"

"Yes, and they're healthy, too, so you don't have to feel guilty eating them. Even so, I couldn't possibly eat the whole batch myself, and I can't think of anyone better to share them with," Claire said honestly. She loved cooking and baking and did love to share what she made with Robby. He was single and not inclined to cook, and Claire always had too much left over, since she was also cooking for one.

Robby's eyes, still on the brownies, narrowed. "Healthy? I don't know ... those paleo prune bars you made last month had an unwanted effect."

Claire chuckled. The prune bars hadn't gone over very well with most people—with the exception of Norma, who wanted her to make another batch to help keep her regular. "Oh, these won't have that effect. No prunes. Just coconut flour, butter, eggs, cacao, vanilla, and maple syrup." Claire lifted a corner of Saran wrap and held the plate up higher so Robby could get a whiff.

"Okay then." Robby stepped back from the door. "Would you like to come in for coffee? I just finished dinner."

"Love to."

Claire followed him into the kitchen, a typical bachelor's kitchen with an old Formica table and chair set that Claire had picked up for him at

Myrna Carson's yard sale the summer Robby bought his house. The walls were devoid of artwork, the countertops bare except for a Keurig coffee maker and a microwave. Claire glanced into the trash and saw a familiar white takeout bag from Chowders. "Takeout again?"

Robby pulled the water reservoir from the Keurig and turned on the water at the sink, talking to Claire over his shoulder. "You know I don't like to cook, and with my schedule, I don't really have time. Take-out is easy, and Chowders's food is good."

Claire pressed her lips together to hide her smile. Robby had created the perfect opening for her to ask about the case. "Yes, I guess your schedule does not lend itself to cooking, but this new case probably won't have you working a lot of extra hours."

She accepted the cup of coffee from him, then glanced up at him over the rim as she took her first sip.

"Oh, I wouldn't say that." Robby ripped two paper towels off the roll that hung under the cabinets and gestured toward the table. They both sat, and Claire removed the Saran wrap from the brownie plate then placed one brownie on a paper towel in front of Robby and one in front of herself.

"I'll bet. I don't see how an old skeleton could be a pressing matter." Claire feigned interest in breaking off a piece of her brownie so Robby wouldn't see the eager gleam in her eye. She thought she'd been subtle in asking the question, but apparently she was not subtle enough.

"Now Auntie, you know I can't tell you any details about an ongoing investigation."

"Of course not. I wouldn't want you to do that. But maybe if you just told me the name of the skeleton, it wouldn't hurt."

Robby looked up sharply. "What makes you think I know who it is?"

"You're a smart boy. I know you've figured out just as I have that it was no pirate skeleton in that chest, and I'm sure you've done the appropriate tests."

Robby sighed. "I suppose it can't hurt to tell you. Once Zambuco starts asking questions tomorrow, the news will be all over the island anyway. The skeleton was Elbert Daniels."

Claire's brows tugged together. "Elbert Daniels? You mean that man who went missing from the island sixty years ago?"

"The same."

"But I thought he fell overboard during a violent storm. They found his boat adrift in Smuggler's Cove the next day, didn't they?"

"You'd remember better than I would. I wasn't even born yet. But that's what the police report said. When a search party couldn't find him, it was ruled an accidental death. He's the only missing person reported in decades, so we compared the dental records, and it was a match." Robby shoved the last of his brownie into his mouth. "These are very good, by the way."

"Thanks," Claire kept her voice light, trying to mask the sinking feeling that was forming in her gut. "Well, I best be going. Early to bed, early to rise."

Robby glanced out the window. "It's only six thirty."

"Right." Claire had already jumped up from the chair and was bringing her cup to the sink. She needed to get home and get to thinking about this new development. If the murder had happened sixty years ago, then there were plenty of islanders still alive who were old enough to be the killer. Zambuco was sure to be turning over every rock to find out who it was, and she needed to keep one step ahead of him. "I have some things to finish up at home before I turn in. Thanks for the company."

Robby saw Claire to the door. She could feel him watching as she hurried away, so she turned and gave him a cheerful wave, a smile plastered on her face as if she hadn't a care in the world. As she turned, that smile snapped into a frown.

She had to figure out her next move quickly. Elbert's killer might still be alive and living on the island ... and thinking they'd gotten away with murder for the past sixty years. When word got out that Elbert's body had been dug up, there was no telling what that person might do.

Chapter 4

Dom stood in front of the Gull View Inn the next afternoon, admiring the wide porch with its white wicker rockers and tables set up with oversized checkerboards. The inn had been attracting guests to the island for more than one hundred fifty years and was known as the go-to place to stay.

The popularity of the inn was no surprise to Dom. Set a little ways up the hill from the town docks, it boasted a charming view of the Atlantic Ocean and the quaint island cove, which was dotted with little shops. The inn had comfortable rooms loaded with antique charm, and the food was delicious. In fact, the smells of clam chowder, fried food, and grilled meat were causing Dom's mouth to water right now.

And it wasn't just the food or ambiance that made the inn popular. The elderly spinster owners were another reason the rooms were full all summer long. Velma and Hazel had run the inn for the past ten years after Velma had inherited it from her father. The two women had to be in their late eighties if they were a day, but they were sharp and full of life. Dom found them delightful.

What he did not find delightful was the vague and mysterious text he'd received from Claire the previous night. He knew that she'd found something out from Robby and was probably giddy with joy in making him wait to find out what it was. Not wanting to appear overeager, Dom had not pressed her, preferring to act as if he was not interested at all. And so here he was standing on the street waiting for Claire with eager anticipation at the news she was about to impart.

Claire's Fiat pulled into a parking spot across the street, and Dom's eyebrows started to tingle as she got out and hurried toward him, a bright gleam of excitement in her eye.

"Good afternoon," Dom said matter-of-factly, as if he wasn't dying to find out what she knew.

"Afternoon." Claire glanced up and down the street to make sure they were alone, then she grabbed his elbow and pulled him aside. "I talked to Robby last night."

Dom nodded. "Yes. And..."

"The victim. It was Elbert Daniels."

Dom's bushy brows drew together as he tried to recall the name. It did not ring a bell. "Is that name supposed to mean something to me?"

"He lived on the island here. When I was a teenager he disappeared during a storm. His boat was found adrift the next day, and everyone thought he'd fallen overboard. Everyone assumed the body was washed out to sea."

"Ahh, I see." Dom nodded. "Well, clearly not everyone assumed he was washed out to sea. At least one person on the island must have known where he really was."

"Yes, and now we need to find out who that person is." Claire tugged Dom toward the inn. "And I think the best place to start is with Velma and Hazel."

Velma and Hazel had been on the island for more than one hundred years, or so it seemed. The two ladies never mentioned their age, but they would certainly have been around when Elbert went missing. Not only that, but it was lunchtime. Dom was hungry, and the Gull View made the best meatball sandwich on the island. The day was looking up.

It was early in the season, and the tourists had yet to hit the island in full force, so Dom and Claire were able to secure one of the best tables next to the large plate-glass windows that overlooked the ocean beyond the expansive outdoor dining deck. Tables were set up outside with colorful blue umbrellas, but it was still a bit chilly in the shade, and Velma and Hazel, who had been delighted to see them, had discouraged outdoor eating.

Velma bustled off to the kitchen to put in their order, and Hazel pulled out a seat and joined them.

"It feels good to take a load off." Hazel glanced around the nearly empty dining room. "Another few weeks and this place will be so crowded I won't be able to find a seat, never mind have time for sittin'."

"It is warming up nicely. The early wave of tourists is sure to descend on us soon," Claire agreed.

Velma appeared, her blue eyes sparkling mischievously as she tossed her order pad on the table, shoved the pencil into her snow-white bun, and sat next to Hazel. "So what brings you two here?"

Dom smiled at her patiently. "We were just hungry for lunch."

Hazel's green eyes narrowed. "Really? You two don't usually eat here. Could it be something about the pirate chest that was dug up yesterday?"

"What do you know about it?" Claire asked as the waitress slid her pear-and-arugula salad in front of her.

"Know? We don't know anything, do we?" Velma looked at Hazel.

"Not a thing. Just that that treasure trunk was dug up at the groundbreaking for the pharmacy and there was an old skeleton inside," Hazel said. "I was thinking it might be Blackbeard or Captain Jack Sparrow."

Velma tilted her head and looked at her friend. "Hazel, Jack Sparrow is a fictional character."

Hazel looked at her sideways. "Oh. I guess you're right." Hazel turned to Dom and Claire. "Well then, who was in the trunk?"

Claire made a big show about glancing around the room. Dom knew the identity of the victim would get out once Zambuco started asking questions, but he figured Claire didn't want to get Robby into trouble if people started finding out before Zambuco let the cat out of the bag. Claire leaned across the table toward Velma and Hazel. "Do you swear not to tell anyone?"

Their eyes sparkled with eager anticipation, and they straightened in their seats. "We do," they said at the same time.

"It was Elbert Daniels."

Hazel gasped. Velma's hand flew up to her chest. "Elbert Daniels? But he was lost at sea."

"Apparently not." Claire stabbed her fork into a chunk of pear.

Velma and Hazel turned to Dom, who was busy working on his meatball sandwich. "Is it true? Why would someone put Elbert into a pirate chest?"

"They wanted to hide the body. Whoever it was must have set his boat adrift, knowing it would appear as if he'd been lost at sea."

"Premeditated murder," Hazel whispered.

"But who would want to murder Elbert? Why, he didn't have an enemy in the world," Velma added.

Dom shrugged. "He must've had at least one. Do either of you know who that might have been?"

They shook their heads. "No. But that does explain something that always bothered me."

"What's that?" Claire asked.

"Elbert was an expert sailor. I never could figure out how he would've been lost at sea or why he would've even taken his boat out in that storm in the first place. It didn't make any sense." Velma's eyes had a faraway look as she glanced out the floor-to-ceiling windows at the ocean.

"That's right." Hazel nodded. "Why, I remember Liz harassing the police to look harder. She knew Elbert would've never just fallen overboard."

"Liz?" Dom asked.

"His wife ... widow," Hazel answered.

"Well, I guess Elbert finally found the treasure he was always looking for," Velma said.

"A lot of good it did him—he wound up inside the chest!" Hazel added.

Velma's eyes darkened. "You don't think someone in the treasure-hunting club did it, do you?"

"Treasure-hunting club?" Claire and Dom said in unison.

Velma looked at Claire. "You're probably too young to remember, but a few of the guys on the island had a treasure-hunting club back then. They believed all the rumors about pirate treasure being buried here on the island."

"Do you remember who was in this club?" Dom asked.

Velma thought for a while and shook her head. "I can't remember...it's been so long. Even his widow has long since left the island. I think she left his treasure-hunting stuff in the locker he had at the storage facility when she left. I don't know what was done with it after that. The treasure-hunting club didn't last long after Elbert disappeared. Maybe now we know why..."

"I remember there were four of them ..." Hazel scrunched up her face and looked up at the ceiling. "I'm pretty sure Benjamin Hill was in it, but I can't remember who else."

Velma pressed her lips together. "Yes, I think Hill was in the Club. I know if I think about it long enough, the rest will come to me." She looked at Dom apologetically. "You know at my age, it takes a while to dig into the memory banks."

Dom nodded, but his mind was not on Velma's words. He was still thinking about Benjamin Hill. Benjamin Hill had been the one who was so vocal about not digging up the site yesterday. Was that because he knew what they would find?

Dom grabbed his napkin and patted his lips. "Well, ladies, this has been quite enjoyable, but I think we are ready for the check. Right, Claire?"

He wasn't surprised to see Claire nodding eagerly, her plate already pushed away. Like Dom, she didn't like to waste time once they had a trail of clues. And while they didn't exactly have a trail of clues, they did have a place to start looking now. And a suspect—Benjamin Hill.

Chapter 5

Claire hurried down the steps of the Gull View Inn, the pear-and-arugula salad barely settled in her stomach. She was excited to be back on the hunt with a trail of clues to follow. She knew that Dom, who was hurrying down the steps at her heels, was just as excited.

"How well do you know Benjamin Hill?" Dom asked. "I think we need to pay a visit."

"Absolutely." Claire crossed to her car and slid into the driver's seat, noting that the sun was just barely slanting over the western section of the island. Just a little past noon. She did want to visit Benjamin, but there was still plenty of time, and she had an idea that might produce better clues.

Velma's mention of the storage facility had piqued Claire's interest. She knew human nature, and when humans had something they didn't want anyone to see but that they wanted to keep, they hid it away in places no one else could get to. Locked places. Like a storage unit. "The storage facility is closer, and I think we might want to make a visit there first to see if there's any record of what was in that unit."

Dom stared at her. "You're choosing physical clues over the body language of a potential suspect?"

"I must be picking up some of your bad habits."

The island had only one storage facility, so it wasn't hard to figure out where to go. It was set off the beaten path, far into the woods. Claire drove a little too fast for the narrow dirt road, but she wasn't worried about speeding tickets—her nephew wouldn't dare ticket her for fear she'd withhold her delicious pies and other desserts.

The stately pine trees and centuries-old oaks whizzed by as she navigated the old roads.

"Watch out for moose," Dom joked. More than a hundred years ago when the first islanders built their camps, there had been a large population of moose. They had run amuck, so to speak, which was how the island had gotten its name. These days, one rarely saw the majestic creatures, whose dwindling population preferred to stick to the undeveloped sections of the island.

The storage facility wasn't much to look at. It had been modernized since its modest beginnings sixty years ago, with the owners adding concrete structures and metal doors.

Naturally Claire knew the owner, Marcy Dodds, the second generation to run the facility. Marcy lived in the ramshackle house at the edge of the property and, since the storage facility was infrequently visited, she didn't have normal office hours, preferring to run over and open up when she saw a car drive in. Which made it odd that the office was open now, the light on and Marcy's rotund figure bustling around inside.

"Someone must be here." Claire drove past the upper parking lot to the first row of units. Maybe it was a coincidence that someone was here, but Claire didn't believe much in coincidence.

There was someone there, and their car was parked around at the end of the first row of units: a shiny new Volvo.

"Isn't that Jane's car?" Dom asked.

"Yes, I believe it is." Claire didn't remember Jane mentioning she had a storage unit, but then they'd been friends for so long it could have been something she'd said in passing years ago that Claire had long forgotten about. Or it could be fairly recent—Jane's mother's dementia had recently worsened, and she'd moved her to an expensive assisted-living facility on the mainland. Jane had moved into the family home and sold her own place, so it made sense she'd need a storage unit to hold the excess items while she

56

sorted through seven decades of memories at her parents' house.

The door to the large unit was open, and Claire could see it was packed to the brim. Jane was weaving her way down a narrow aisle, her attention riveted on a small cardboard box in her hands. Claire's approach must have startled Jane, as the woman jerked her head up and clutched the box to her chest.

"Claire! You scared me." Jane glanced nervously over her shoulder into the storage unit, then her eyes drifted back to Claire and then over to Dom. "What are you two doing here?"

"Actually, were following up a lead on the body that was found in the trunk yesterday," Claire said.

Jane's brow creased. "You're investigating that?"

Well, we can't let Zambuco do it and get it all wrong. Claire did not voice her thoughts. Even though Jane hadn't confessed anything to her, Claire knew there was something between her and Zambuco, and she didn't want to hurt her friend's feelings.

"We are," Dom said.

Jane pulled down the storage unit door and slipped on the lock. Over her shoulder she said,

"But isn't it a three-hundred-year-old murder? How do you expect to be able to solve it?"

"Actually, it isn't. The victim turned out to be Elbert Daniels," Claire said.

Jane sucked in a breath. Straightening from the task of putting on the lock, she wobbled on her feet.

"Are you all right, Jane?" Claire put her hand on Jane's arm to steady her.

Jane waved her off. "I'm fine. It's just...it's shocking, that's all. I remember Elbert from when I was a little girl. But I thought he drowned in a boat accident."

"That's what everyone thought." Claire couldn't shake the feeling that Jane knew more than she was letting on. Maybe it was only the fact that she'd known him as a child, but judging by her body language, Claire had a pretty good idea that Jane might have some information for them. She waited patiently, but Jane didn't say any more.

"How did you know Elbert?" Dom asked after a few seconds.

"I didn't really know him. I was young at the time. What would you say we were, around ten years old, Claire?" Jane turned to Claire, who nodded. "Anyway, I think he was a friend of my dad. I remember meeting him once or twice."

That explained it. Jane's dad had died of a heart attack when they were teens, and it always upset Jane to think about him even after all these years. Bringing up Elbert must remind her of her father. Claire could sympathize, having lost her father a couple years ago.

"But what brings you here though? Did Elbert have a storage unit? I'm sure it wouldn't still be occupied if he did," Jane said.

"He did have one, according to Velma. We're just checking the facts, figuring maybe there was some kind of record of what he had. His widow left the island soon after his disappearance, and we don't know if she even cared what was in it. If the bill wasn't paid, the contents would have been auctioned off, and there might be an inventory record of the contents. Maybe we can find a clue in that inventory." Dom shrugged. "You never know."

"I'll leave you guys to it, then," Jane said. Claire noticed the color had come back to her cheeks, and she seemed cheery enough as she waved good-bye and got into her car. Claire admonished herself for being suspicious of her dearest friend. Sometimes she let her investigative instincts get the best of her.

Dom watched her car drive away then glanced at the storage unit door. "Did she seem unsettled to you?"

"With good reason." Claire came to her friend's defense. "Her dad died when she was young, and remembering back to those days probably reminds her of losing him. She might've even been in the storage unit getting memorabilia from him. Maybe something to bring to her mother at Greenbriar Manor, the assisted-living home on the mainland."

Dom's face turned thoughtful. "I suppose that would do it. It's not easy losing a loved one."

"That's true." Claire didn't want to let Dom dwell on his sad memories. Best to get on with the investigation. That would bring the spark back to his eye and the spring to his step. "Come on, let's catch Marcy in the office before she goes back home."

They walked to the office. As they opened the door, Marcy looked up from her seat at the desk on the other side of the counter, her head barely visible behind the tall countertop.

Upon recognizing them, she shot out of her chair, which didn't make her a heck of a lot taller. Claire herself was almost five feet seven inches and judged Marcy to be a good half a foot shorter. Marcy's pudgy face beamed with a welcoming smile. "So many visitors today! What can I do for you?"

"Hi, Marcy," Claire said. "I hope you can help us. We heard that Elbert Daniels had a storage unit here. I don't suppose you happen to know what was in there? Do you know anything about it?"

Marcy nodded. "Of course. You're not the first people to be asking about that unit this week."

Dom's brows shot up in surprise. "We're not? Who else was asking?"

"I don't know her name. She was new to the island, I suppose. Sweet young girl. Tall with dark-brown hair."

Great, Claire thought. That kind of description would fit half the population. "Did she have any distinguishing marks?"

"Distinguishing marks?"

"You know, birthmarks, something unusual about her?"

Marcy shook her head. "No. I wasn't really looking."

"So what did you tell her about the unit?" Dom asked. "And what happened to the contents?"

"Oh, we still have the contents. Daddy always had a rule that unless all the units were rented and a new customer needed the space, we kept the contents of the units that people didn't pay for."

Marcy shrugged. "He always did have a soft spot for his fellow islanders, and he figured they might make good on the bill someday. He hated to get rid of their stuff, and if we couldn't rent the space to someone else, then it wasn't really hurting us. Daddy always thought that one day Liz or one of her children would come back and want to see what Elbert had stored in there."

"Do you think maybe we could take a look?" Dom asked.

Marcy narrowed her eyes. "Well, I don't know if that would be right ..."

"Technically, if the bill has not been paid, I'd imagine the contents now belong to the storage facility. Most general storage contracts have that clause to allow the owner to sell off the contents to make up for nonpayment. I'm sure your contract is no different. So legally, you'd be free to show it to whoever you want," Dom said.

"It could be vitally important," Claire added.

"Vitally important? Wait a minute, you mean this has something to do with the body that was found yesterday?" Marcy's voice rose with the excitement of being involved in a murder investigation.

"It may."

"But I thought that was an old pirate."

Claire sighed and glanced at Dom, who nodded. "I suppose the truth will be out all over the island soon, but don't let Zambuco know we told you. The body was Elbert Daniels."

Marcy's hand flew up to her face. "Oh my. You mean he didn't die in that boat accident?"

"No, and you can see why it's important that we see what he had stored. There could be a clue to his killer in there."

"Of course." Marcy turned around to a row of keys that was tacked up on the board behind her and plucked one off, then came around the counter and headed toward the door, motioning for them to follow. They hurried to the last row of storage units and watched as she bent over and slipped the key into an old, rusted lock.

She grunted and jammed the key in, yanking and twisting it. "This unit doesn't get opened often, and the lock is almost rusted shut."

"Let me see." Dom squatted down to help her. After a few seconds of fiddling, the lock clicked open, and he lifted up the squealing metal door.

Claire eagerly peered inside, her excitement plummeting to disappointment.

"It's empty."

Confusion registered on Marcy's face. "I don't understand. The equipment was still here two weeks ago when I did the monthly check to make sure there were no leaks or mice, and I have the only key. Well, the only key besides the one Elbert had."

"What about the girl who asked about it?" Claire asked.

Marcy shook her head. "No, she never even came to it, as far as I know. I verified he did have a unit here, and she thanked me and drove off."

Dom walked into the unit, and Claire watched, fascinated, as he inspected the floor, the corners, the walls. She had no idea what he found so interesting—to her it was just an empty space—but to Dom, apparently, there were clues to be found.

She could see the scrapes, impressions, rusted spots, and dark areas that stained the floor from decades of equipment storage. Dom scuffed the floor in the corner with his toe, turning over some peculiar-looking red pebbles. He bent and picked a few up, slipping them into his pocket.

"Well, I guess there's not much in the way of clues here." Dom patted his right brow then turned and met Claire's gaze. Her gut sank when she saw her own disturbing thoughts reflected in his eyes.

Someone didn't want anyone to see what had been in here. But who? And why?

Chapter 6

Benjamin Hill lived on the more affluent side of the island in a large estate with a panoramic ocean view and professionally manicured grounds.

"So this is how the other half lives," Dom said as the tires of Claire's Fiat crunched on the pebble driveway. He got out of the car and scuffed the gravel with his toe. Claire's questioning look told him that she was thinking about the pebbles from the storage unit, but Dom shook his head. "Not the right color or size."

"Now remember, let's act like we're just talking about island events," Claire cautioned as they approached the imposing wooden door.

"Agreed. We don't want to let on that the body was Elbert Daniels. We don't want to tip Benjamin off if he knows something. He'll find out soon enough who was in the trunk when word gets around the island."

Claire knocked on the door, and a few minutes later, it opened to reveal Allen Hill, surprise registering as he recognized them. "Claire? Dom? What are you doing here?"

"We've come to pay a visit to your grandfather. I was most concerned about him yesterday. A man of his age shouldn't be getting all riled up like that," Claire said.

"That's very nice of you. Grandpa is fine, though." Allen didn't invite them in. In fact, he looked like he was about to shoo them away.

Claire stepped up to the threshold. "Oh, that's good. Is he willing to receive visitors?"

Allen glanced over his shoulder into the house. "Well ... I don't—"

"Who's that, Allen?" Benjamin's voice boomed down the hall.

"It's Claire Watson and Dominic Benedetti," Allen replied.

"Oh? Well, show them in. I could use some company."

Allen hesitated then swung the door wide, allowing Claire and Dom entrance to the marble-and-mahogany foyer. Dom took his time looking around, his trained eye cataloging everything from the ornately carved round table in the center of the foyer to the arrangements of white flowers on the consoles against the walls. He was used to studying every crime scene for clues and, though this wasn't a crime scene, it was a habit he could not turn off.

67

"This way." Allen turned down a hallway, and they followed. A row of old gilt-framed paintings lined the walls. Hill ancestors, no doubt. One of the paintings was tilted slightly to the right, and Dom paused in front of it, tapping the bottom gently with his index finger, adjusting the angle so it lined up perfectly with the rest of the paintings.

Claire and Allen were just entering a room at the end of the hall. Dom hurried to join them and found himself in a handsomely decorated room lined with bookcases on three walls. Golden sunlight spilled in from the nine-foot-tall windows, highlighting rectangles of color on the jewel-toned Oriental rug.

An enormous stone fireplace took up the entire wall across from them, and two tufted leather sofas were arranged in the middle of the room facing each other. On one of the sofas sat Benjamin Hill, a plaid blanket over his lap despite the warm spring air. Dom noticed how small and frail he looked today. Apparently all the huffing and puffing at the pharmacy site the previous day had worn him out.

"Come in, come in." Benjamin gestured toward the sofa across from him, and Dom did as instructed, sinking into the soft, buttery leather. He wondered how often Benjamin got visitors. Not very often, judging by how excited he was to see them. Allen probably drove most of them away.

"Grandfather, you know you're supposed to be resting, so your guests can't stay long." Allen shot a pointed look at Dom and Claire as he fussed with the blanket on Benjamin's lap.

"Oh, posh. A little visit ain't gonna kill me." Benjamin pushed Allen away, and Allen sighed then resorted to hovering behind the sofa.

"We won't stay too long," Claire said then added, "Boy, that was some spectacle yesterday morning with the treasure chest."

"Yeah, I bet you weren't expecting anything like that when you were protesting," Dom added.

Benjamin narrowed his eyes. "No. Certainly not. Though I'd heard the rumors of buried pirate treasure since I was a boy."

"We all have. Didn't there used to be a treasure-hunting club on the island?" Claire asked.

"There was. But we've been disbanded a long time."

"I think I vaguely remember about it," Claire lied. "It broke up right around the time Elbert Daniels fell overboard all those years ago, didn't it?"

Benjamin's eyes narrowed at the mention of Elbert Daniels. His gaze drifted to the window as if he were trying to conjure up old, buried memories from sixty years ago. "Now that you mention it, it was about that time."

"That was a long time ago," Allen cut in. "Do we have to dredge up my grandpa's old memories? I don't want him getting upset."

"I'm not made of sugar, boy! It does me good to remember. Though my memory is a little fuzzy now." Benjamin lapsed into reflective silence then started and whipped his head around to look at Allen still hovering behind him. "Where are your manners, boy? Aren't you going to offer our guests some coffee?"

Allen raised a brow at Dom and Claire, who both nodded.

"I take mine with cream," Dom added as Allen hesitantly left the room. Dom was happy to have some time to talk to Benjamin alone. It seemed that Allen wanted to stifle his grandfather's memories, and Dom felt that Benjamin would be more inclined to talk without Allen in the room.

"Tell us more about this treasure-hunting club," Dom said. "It must've been exciting. Did you ever find any good treasure?"

Benjamin snorted. "Not hardly. We dug up a few old rings, brooches, worthless coins. But it never did amount to much."

"Really? I thought maybe you amassed all your fortune from treasure," Dom teased, spreading his hand to indicate the lavishly decorated room.

Benjamin bristled. "I should say not. I made the Hill family fortune trading commodities."

"None of the other members of the treasure-hunting club became rich," Claire pointed out. "Certainly not Elbert Daniels."

Benjamin's gaze snapped to Claire. "No, no one became rich from the treasure hunting. It was just a lark."

"A fun hobby, right?" Dom asked.

His light tone seemed to appease Benjamin. "That's right."

"So, it was you and Elbert Daniels in the club. I can't remember who else ..." Claire let her voice drift off, and Dom knew she was leading Benjamin to fill in the other members.

"Gosh, that was a long time ago. There were a few of us. Quentin Crane and Billy Wilkinson and ..."

Benjamin paused, and Dom couldn't tell if it was because of fading memories or that there was another member he didn't want to mention.

"And?" Dom prompted.

"It doesn't matter now." Benjamin's voice turned gruff. "The only two left of us are Quentin and me. And we didn't find any treasure, for all our digging."

"Then you didn't try to dig up the pharmacy lot?" Claire asked.

"Sure we did. We dug holes all over the darn island. I guess we just weren't lucky enough. Never found anything valuable, that's for sure."

"Then why protest so hard against the pharmacy if you didn't think there was treasure there?"

Benjamin's face hardened. "I didn't say if I thought there was or wasn't treasure there. The club obviously never dug in the right spot. But my protest was about more than just some treasure. It's about these newfangled changes that are turning the island into a city. I can't abide that. Pretty soon my beautiful island will be ruined."

"Now Grandpa, don't go getting upset." Allen shoved the coffee tray he'd been holding onto a table and rushed over to Benjamin, shooting daggers at Claire and Dom on the way. "You know the doctor said you should be resting."

Dom stood. He didn't really want coffee, and he figured they'd learned everything they could from Benjamin. "We don't want to overstay our welcome. If you are supposed to be resting, then we'll take our leave."

"But Allen just brought coffee," Benjamin said.

Claire patted him on the knee. "That's okay, Ben, we'll come back and have coffee another time."

"We can show ourselves out," Dom said, already halfway across the room.

In the car, Claire said, "I don't know if that went well or not. I couldn't translate Benjamin's reaction to the mention of Elbert, and I have no idea if he knew that the pharmacy groundbreaking might have dug up that chest."

Dom's brow ticked up. "Really? And here I thought you could tell everything from a person's body language."

Claire huffed. "Well, either Benjamin has actually forgotten, or he's a very good actor, or he knew nothing about Elbert being buried there in that chest."

Dom glanced back at the house as Claire pulled out of the driveway. "I would have liked to have asked him more questions, but I felt like the interrogation—I mean interview—had run its course."

"Yeah, I don't think we were going to get much more out of him. And Allen didn't help matters much."

"He seemed reluctant to let Benjamin say too much."

"Well, at least he verified that there was a treasure club and Benjamin, Elbert, Bill, and Quentin were in it, even if they didn't dig up any valuable treasure."

Dom pressed his lips together. "That's the part that I would have liked to question him more about. It doesn't ring true. I don't know if that chest they dug up yesterday once had valuable treasure in it, but I do know that someone dug that chest up sixty years ago and stuffed Elbert into it. And if that person wasn't Benjamin Hill—who was protesting the dig so vehemently—then who was it?"

Chapter 7

Claire and Dom arranged to meet the next morning at Chowders before the rest of the breakfast gang arrived. They wanted to discuss the clues in private before everyone else started pumping them for information. Even though they weren't working for the police anymore, they both still believed that some clues should be held back, as general knowledge of them could adversely affect the investigation.

Though anxious to move forward with the investigation, Claire had needed the time to mull over what they had discovered. Besides, she always did her best work after a good night's sleep, with her morning elixir of apple cider vinegar and lemon juice powering her brain.

Dom was already waiting in the diner, a half-eaten slice of ricotta pie on the plate in front of him. Claire sat across the table and ordered a red rooibos tea for starters. She'd wait and order her food when the others joined them so she could eat with everyone else.

"That stuff will kill you, you know." Claire pointed to the creamy piece of pie.

"Oh, but what a way to go," Dom mumbled, his mouth full.

Claire's eyes drifted over to the pharmacy lot, which now had yellow crime scene tape around the dark, gaping hole. The bulldozer sat silently beside it, its large shovel resting empty on the ground. Quite a difference from the activity of two mornings ago.

"So, did you have any revelations last night?" Claire ripped open the small teabag packet, pulled the bag out, and dunked it in the steaming water Sarah had already poured into her mug.

Dom shook his head. "Nothing that you probably already didn't think of. We don't have many clues to go on."

Claire leaned across the table, lowering her voice to just above a whisper. "But we do have the names of a few suspects. The other members of the treasure-hunting club. Bill Wilkinson passed a few years ago, but Quentin is still alive and living at Greenbriar Manor."

"Yes, we must speak to Quentin ... and find out who the other person was. I got the distinct impression that Benjamin was about to name someone else yesterday."

"I noticed that too, but I doubt Allen will let us talk to him again so soon. I ran into Allen at Carter's Market last night, and he gave me the hairy eyeball. Mentioned how his grandfather had taken to his bed after we left. I got the distinct impression we would not be welcome at the Hill mansion anytime soon."

"Do you think Allen might suspect that Benjamin was involved in Elbert's death? Maybe that's why he wants to keep us away from him."

"Maybe." Claire took a sip of tea as she thought about it. "I don't know how Allen would know anything about it, though. That happened so long ago, and he wasn't even born yet."

"If only we could find out more about the investigation into Elbert's disappearance, that might give us some clues," Dom suggested.

"I doubt Zambuco will share any of that with us. Robby might let us look at some of the old records, though I doubt it now that the case has been reopened."

Dom sighed and pushed his empty plate aside. Reaching into his pocket, he took out the red pebble and held it in the palm of his hand. "All we really have for physical clues is this pebble."

"Where do you think the pebble came from? Do you think it's from a location where they dug for treasure? Like it got stuck on the bottom of their equipment or something?"

"I don't know. These rocks are ornamental. I did some research last night, and they are not indigenous to the area, so they must have been brought in for some particular use."

"You mean like in a garden or a fish tank or something?"

"Yes, but not the Zen garden. These are not the same types of rocks they use for that."

Claire sat back in her seat, the warm mug cupped in her hand. She couldn't recall any garden, pond, or other area on the island with red rocks. Then again, she hadn't been looking for them. "Ornamental, you say? I noticed Benjamin Hill's house had nicely landscaped gardens. Maybe they use stones like that in one of them."

Dom got that faraway look on his face that Claire knew meant he was remembering what he'd seen at Benjamin's house. "I didn't see any decorative rocks there, but we only saw the front entry and sides. There could be something out back."

"We'll have to keep our eyes open. In the meantime, can we agree that our next course of action is to question Quentin Crane? Maybe he remembers something that Benjamin didn't mention."

"At the very least, we can see if their stories line up."

Dom's eyes flicked to the door, and he snapped his fist closed and shoved it into his pocket. "Here comes Jane. The others will be here soon. We won't mention the pebbles to anyone, agreed?"

"Agreed." Claire looked at her watch. "Let's table the discussion and agree to take the two p.m. ferry out to Greenbriar Manor."

Jane pulled out the seat next to Claire, her gaze falling to the crumbs on Dom's plate. "Looks like you two were here bright and early. Did someone change the breakfast time?"

"No, we just met to talk about the investigation," Claire said.

Jane's back stiffened. "Oh, that's the discussion you just said you wanted to table. What have you discovered?"

"Not very much. I gather that Zambuco is investigating, and by now everyone likely knows that the victim was Elbert and that this is not a three-hundred-year-old murder we're dealing with." Claire had heard the snatches of conversation from the other diners. It was clear the Mooseamuck Island grapevine was working overtime.

"And do you have a clue as to who did it?" Jane asked.

"Not really. We don't have any motive yet," Dom said.

Jane's eyes narrowed. "Well, he must have been killed because of the treasure. Don't you think?"

Claire shrugged. "Maybe. Maybe not." She slid her eyes over to Jane. Was Jane unusually interested in the murder, or was it her imagination? Maybe she was scouting out clues for Zambuco.

"So tell us, how did you know Elbert?" Dom asked.

"I told you, I didn't really know him. My dad knew him. He used to come to the house with Bill Wilkinson and drink beer with my dad."

"And what did they talk about? Treasure hunting?"

"No, it was always boring grown-up stuff. I eavesdropped once, and it was all about collectables. My dad had a big baseball card collection, and I guess maybe the other guys collected stuff, too. It was boring, so I didn't pay much attention to them."

Sarah came to the table, and Jane put in her order just as the other Mooseamuck Island breakfast regulars filed in the door. Claire settled back in her chair, giving Sarah her own order for oatmeal with cranberries.

Across from her, Dom was looking at Jane and smoothing his eyebrow. Had he noticed that Jane seemed overly interested, too? Jane's interest probably meant nothing. Heck, if the snippets of conversation she'd been overhearing in the diner behind her were any indication, most of the island seemed overly interested in who killed Elbert.

But Jane had brought up one good point about motive. If Elbert had been killed because someone didn't want to share the treasure that had been in the chest, then where, exactly, was the treasure now?

Chapter 8

Dom's first thought when he saw the lavish brick-and-concrete building of Greenbriar Manor was that it must cost an arm and a leg to live there. He knew little about the exclusive assisted-living facility except that it was fairly new and offered residents highly skilled medical care, gourmet meals, and the option to roam in and out of the facility as they pleased.

Dom and Claire had taken the ferry over using Claire's Fiat because it was small and easy to maneuver on the boat. As she pulled into the parking spot, Dom took note of the fine details of the building. Fancy brickwork over the doors and windows, carved moldings along the edge of the roof, and meticulously groomed gardens told him that this was no run-of-the-mill operation. A large covered portico offered a safe place to offload passengers, and the lobby looked to be finely outfitted with upscale furnishings.

"Isn't this where Jane has her mother? Must be quite expensive," Dom said.

"Yes, Lila is here. I'd like to stop in and say hi while we are here, if you don't mind." Claire pocketed her key and glanced at the large building. "I know Jane wanted her mom to have the best care, and this is the best around, but honestly I don't know how Jane can afford it. Maybe her mother had money stashed away."

Dom couldn't remember a time when Jane wasn't worried about money ... at least until about a year ago. That was when she started showing up with new outfits and the new car. He didn't think her mother had any either. Had she come into money? If she had, wouldn't she have told Claire?

Thoughts of the empty treasure chest and the unusual way Jane had been acting drifted through his mind, but he quickly dismissed his suspicions. How could Jane's sudden increase in wealth possibly have anything to do with a treasure that was unearthed sixty years ago?

"I wonder what was actually in the treasure chest. I mean before Elbert," Claire said as if echoing his thoughts.

"It could have been filled with gold or pirate plunder, or it could have been empty. We don't know if the treasure was the motive for Elbert's death, but I do think we should research any newfound wealth that might've come to someone on the island during that time." Dom opened the car door and got out, stretching his back as he did.

"Do you think there could have been enough in there to make the killer wealthy?" Claire asked over the top of the Fiat.

"We can't say for sure, but it's definitely a stone we should not leave unturned."

Visions of Benjamin Hill's estate flitted through Dom's mind. Had Benjamin really amassed that wealth by trading commodities? And then there was Jane's sudden increase in wealth, not to mention Quentin Crane, who was also one of the treasure-hunting members and now resided right here in the exclusive assisted-living facility. So many suspects, but which one was the killer? Or was it someone else entirely?

Although gray clouds threatened on the horizon, the day was warm and pleasant, the air lightly scented with the promise of spring rain. Several residents were taking advantage of the calm before the storm by sitting outside, some on the stone benches that dotted the garden and others in white rockers on a large porch to the west.

Claire stopped suddenly. "That's Quentin Crane over there."

Dom followed her gaze to see two men. One was sitting on a stone bench. He assumed that was Quentin. Though he knew Quentin was in his nineties, he possessed the vim and vigor of a younger man. He sat on the bench, his body erect, his large hand resting atop a mahogany cane with an enormous lion's head at the top, his face eager. Quentin Crane was no frail, senile old man.

The other man appeared to be in his sixties and was standing with his back to them. As Dom watched them talk, a sinking feeling came over him, and when the man turned, his suspicions were confirmed.

"Darn! It's Zambuco," Claire said.

"Looks like he's following the same trail of clues that we are."

Just then, Zambuco spotted them, his dark eyes narrowing.

"Shoot! He's seen us. We might as well go over and act like we're here on a regular visit." Claire started in Zambuco's direction, and Dom followed.

"What are you two doing here?" Zambuco demanded. Dom was surprised to see the man was once again fairly well dressed. Typically he had crumbs on his tie or stains on his shirt. His clothes were usually rumpled, and the colors always clashed. Today, he was neat as a pin. Dom had noticed the lingering looks between Zambuco and Jane. Was his new attire Jane's influence?

"We're here to visit some of the older islanders," Claire said. "I like to keep in touch."

Zambuco nodded his head slowly, assessing Claire as if he didn't believe her. "That may be true, but I hope that asking questions about a certain treasure chest that was found with a body in it won't be part of your visit."

Claire feigned surprise. "Of course not. Contrary to what you might think, our whole existence isn't about butting into your investigations."

"Really? It sure seems that way." Zambuco leaned in toward them, his thick brows working up and down like caterpillars munching on a leaf. "I'll warn you only once this time. You have no authority to be looking into this case."

An unexpected voice interrupted him. "It's okay, Frank. They're here with me."

Dom turned around to see Jane pushing an elderly woman in a wheelchair. A jolt of suspicion ran through his mind. Was it any coincidence she'd decided to visit her mother here at the same exact time he and Claire had planned to visit Quentin? He remembered her coming up on them at Chowders when they were discussing their visit. She must have overheard them. Then again, this time of year, the ferry only made four trips, so it stood to reason Jane would take the same ferry out.

At the sight of Jane, Zambuco's face softened. "Hello, Jane."

Jane nodded and smiled then bent down to speak in Lila's ear. "Mom, do you remember Frank?"

"Oh yes, yes," Lila said uncertainly.

From the look on Jane's face and Lila's tone and blank look of unrecognition, Dom didn't think she did remember. He wondered when and why Zambuco would have met Jane's mom.

"And you know Claire and Dom," Jane said.

Lila's cloudy eyes showed a dim spark of recognition. "Of course. How are you both?"

Claire bent down and kissed Lila's papery cheek. "Very well, Mrs. Kuhn. How are you?"

Lila smiled. "I can't complain."

Zambuco cleared his throat. "Well, I'll be on my way. I have lots to do on the official investigation." At the word "official," he cast a warning glare at Claire before walking away.

Jane watched him leave. "It's just an act, you know. I'm sure he doesn't really object to you investigating."

"Well, it's a pretty good act, then, because it sure as heck seems like he does," Claire said.

Quentin had gotten up from the bench and was making his way to the entrance of the building. Dom nudged Claire with his elbow and jerked his head in that direction.

Claire bent down to Lila's level. "It was lovely to see you, Mrs. Kuhn. I'll come back and visit with Jane sometime soon." She straightened and addressed Jane. "Thanks for saving us from Zambuco's wrath. I'll let you get on with your visit with your mom. Maybe we can come back together next week?"

"That would be lovely." Jane's smile didn't quite reach her eyes, and Dom wondered if it was worry over her mother or something else. He didn't have much time to ponder, though, as Quentin had already disappeared into the building.

By the time they got inside, Quentin was halfway down the main hall. Dom hurried behind Claire, his investigator's eye taking note of the interior décor, which could be summed up as lavishly tasteful: large flower arrangements, bulky mahogany furniture, and pleasant muted colors on the walls and rugs.

It smelled deliciously of roasting meat, which Dom figured must have been the prime rib he'd seen written on the menu board he'd passed on the way in. Not like any nursing home he'd ever been in. Then again, this wasn't a nursing home.

Maybe he should enquire as to the costs in preparation for his own golden years?

"Please, can I take some of your hours?" The begging voice drifted out from a small library room off the main hallway. Inside, a tall brunette wearing maroon scrubs—perhaps a nurse or an aide that worked at the facility—was pleading with an older bleached blonde. "I didn't realize how expensive it was going to be to live up here, and if I don't get a few more hours, I'm afraid I won't have any place to stay."

The girl reminded Dom of his daughter, and he felt a pang of sympathy for her. But her lack of hours was not his problem. He couldn't solve it for her, and his target was getting away. Dom continued past the room, picking up the pace.

They finally caught up with the older man, and Claire touched his elbow as they came alongside him.

"Hey, Quentin?"

He wheeled around to look at her, the angry frown on his face giving way to a small smile as he recognized her. "Claire Watkins?"

"Yes, it's me. How are you?"

"Just ducky. What brings you here?" Quentin leaned on his cane, facing Claire, his suspicious eyes flicking from her to Dom.

"We were wondering if we could talk to you," Claire said.

Quentin's eyes narrowed. "To me? What about?"

"We saw you talking to Zambuco, and we wanted to find out what he was asking." Dom leaned toward the old man as if sharing a confidence. Claire had once told him that people would usually open up if they thought they were in on a secret. He'd tried it more than a few times and always found it to work. Though he wouldn't admit to her that he'd adopted one of her tactics, he used it quite frequently. "We have our suspicions about him."

Quentin mulled it over then nodded his head. "We can talk in there." He pointed to a large, empty room with the end of his cane.

They sat in three wingback chairs grouped around a low, round table. The chairs were of good quality, upholstered in a soft tan microfiber. Dom chose the seat farthest away from the roaring fireplace. Who needed a fire in this warm spring weather?

"So, what's your beef with Zambuco?" Quentin asked. "I never did like that guy. Arrogant and pushy."

Dom nodded. "Yes, he is. We're a little worried about his questions concerning the treasure-hunting group. We heard you were a member."

Quentin looked at them suspiciously. "Yeah, what of it?"

"We just want to make sure Zambuco doesn't unfairly accuse anyone from that club. We know that Benjamin Hill, Elbert Daniels, Billy Wilkinson, and you were members, but we heard there was a fifth member as well. Do you know who that was?" Claire asked.

"There was a fifth member, but he didn't go on the treasure digs or anything. He was a silent partner. Financed us. I don't know who he was, though. Only Billy Wilkinson knew."

"You mean this silent partner bought the equipment that you used for your hunts and that Elbert Daniels kept?"

Quentin shrugged. "Yep. Elbert had the most space to keep it. But the equipment—metal detectors, shovels, picks, and the like—belonged to the whole group. The silent partner sprang for it, and then we paid him back a little at a time with money from our recoveries."

They were interrupted by the same aide Dom had seen begging for more hours as they'd walked down the hallway. A quick glance at her name tag told him her name was Diane Randall. Now that he had a closer look, he could see she didn't look anything like his daughter other than her height and hair color.

"Hello." She smiled at Dom and Claire. "I hope you're having a nice visit, Quentin. I wanted to remind you about your physical therapy at four. I don't want you to miss another session. You need to keep your legs strong so you can still go on all your outings."

"I won't forget." Quentin patted the hand that Diane had resting lightly on his shoulder and smiled up at her then turned to Claire and Dom with a gleam in his eye. "I keep this little lady entertained with all my treasure-hunting stories, now don't I?"

"Yes, I always love to hear them," Diane said with a tight smile. By the look on her face, Dom didn't think she really did love to hear them. A young girl like her probably found the old man's ramblings boring. Dom wondered if his daughter thought all of his stories of past cases were boring, too.

"I'm sure they are fascinating," Dom said. "But what do you mean your outings? Don't you have to stay inside the manor?"

Quentin made a face. "This isn't a prison. It's just an assisted living. I get my medication, physical therapy, and meals, but I'm free to come and go as I please. Lucky thing, too, or I'd never know what was going on outside these walls. It's hard enough to stay in touch with the happenings in the real world. I feel disconnected sometimes."

"That's right, Quentin is free to visit his friends, go shopping, do whatever he wants. But if he doesn't do his physical therapy, his mobility will be severely limited. Especially with those bad knees," Diane lectured. "Now I'll let you continue your visit. I have to check on Mrs. McDonald."

As Diane walked away, her squeaking shoes drew Dom's attention. The thick rubber soles screeched on the marble floor, and then he watched in amazement as a small red pebble fell from the bottom of her shoe.

"What's that?" His words stopped her, and she turned, frowning down at the pebble which Dom was pointing to.

"Oh, those are stones from the meditation garden off the east wing. It's a wonderful and serene place. A lot of the members like to go there and watch the sunrises. But my shoes have such thick tread that the stones get caught in them. Happens to most of the nurses here. There's stones all over the place." She leaned in as if sharing a confidence with Dom. "The cleaning people don't appreciate it very much."

"I'll bet they don't," Dom said, still staring down at the rock as Diane bent to pick it up. He glanced over at Claire. "I think we need to visit this meditation garden."

Claire was already up out of her seat. "Me too. I love meditating." She looked back down at Quentin. "Well, it was nice talking to you, Quentin, enjoy your therapy."

"Oh, I will." Quentin had a wide smile on his face as he watched them leave, but as Dom turned away, he thought he detected a note of unfriendliness in that smile. Maybe Quentin didn't appreciate them dredging up memories of the old treasure-hunting club.

They walked down the east wing and through the glass doors to a beautiful garden area that opened to a view of the Atlantic Ocean. The garden was circular, with granite benches in the center and rows of flowers on the edge. Paths paved with red pebbles meandered through the flowers. Dom bent down and scooped up some of the pebbles then took the one out of his pocket and compared them. They were an exact match.

He looked up at Claire then out across the ocean, where the dark-gray clouds rolling toward them indicated a storm was brewing. "These pebbles may not have been left in the storage unit from the sixty-year-old equipment, like we first thought. They may have been left by whoever it was that took the equipment more recently. Someone who didn't want anyone else to see what was in there."

Chapter 9

Dom wanted to get back to the island before the rain started. It was no fun riding the ferry in a thunderstorm. From the passenger seat of Claire's Fiat, he stared out the windshield, watching the boat pull into the dock and wondering what their next step should be.

"We can't be sure those rocks came from Greenbriar Manor," Claire said. "There must be plenty of other places that use those rocks."

"I'm sure there are. Maybe we can find that place that sells those rocks and find out if they have sold to any other place near or on the island," Dom suggested.

"Right, because otherwise it would mean that someone from Greenbriar might be connected to Elbert's death. I mean assuming they cleaned out the storage unit to get rid of evidence." Claire turned to Dom. "Do you think it's someone that lives there, like Quentin?"

"It could be. Or it could be one of the staff members."

"Right, or even a visitor..."

Like Jane.

"It's too bad only Bill Wilkinson knew who the silent partner was. That might be a better angle to pursue than those rocks," Dom said as the ferry staff lowered the ramp and Claire navigated the Fiat off the boat. "I wonder if he would have told his wife who it was. Spouses often share confidences."

Claire snapped on the wipers, peering out the windshield. "He might have ... the Wilkinson place is on the way to your condo."

"And it's a nice rainy day for a visit."

Claire turned up Israel Head Hill Road. Mari Wilkinson lived in one of the original cottages near the bottom of the hill. The cottage was old but had been updated over the years and was neat as a pin. They knocked on the cheerful yellow door and were greeted by Mari, a petite white-haired woman in her early eighties. She'd been much younger than Bill, and though she looked like a wind could blow her away, Dom noticed she still seemed quite chipper.

She looked pleased to see them and invited them in, leading them to a kitchen with gleaming stainless steel appliances and granite counters. They sat at the antique oak table and listened to the rain pelt the windows as she put on water for tea.

"So much excitement lately. I'm getting so many visitors," Mari said.

"Really? Like who?" Claire asked with a sideways glance at Dom.

Marie looked up at the ceiling. "Well, Jane Kuhn just visited me, and then there was that nice detective..."

Dom's brow twitched at the words "nice detective," but he kept his mouth shut and accepted the dainty tea cup from Mari.

"...and Ben and Quentin, of course. They're so good to keep coming to visit even though Bill is long gone."

Claire reached out to lay her hand on Mari's arm. "I know how hard it is to lose a loved one. If you ever need someone to talk to ..."

Mari settled into one of the chairs, her small hand around her own steaming teacup. "Thank you, but I'm okay. He's been gone a long time."

Dom hated to capitalize on talking about a dead loved one, but he saw his chance to turn the conversation to Bill and, hopefully, the treasure-hunting club. "I didn't have the chance to know Bill. I understand he was sick for several years?"

"Oh, yes. Old age, you know. It gets the best of us," Mari said.

Dom frowned at her pointed look. Did she think he was old? He was only in his late sixties.

"I heard he was something of an adventurer in his youth," Dom continued.

Mari laughed. "If you can call it that. He always thought he would make a big discovery. Was even part of a treasure-hunting club here on the island."

"You don't sound like you approve," Claire said.

"Well, he spent a lot of time and money and never did find any treasure. Only a grubby old brooch, and he refused to let me clean it. I must have it around here somewhere ... oh dear, I can't remember where I put it. Maybe in my jewelry box ..."

"It's okay. We don't need to see it," Claire said, obviously trying to soothe the flustered Mari.

Dom raised his eyebrows at Claire in an unspoken, We don't?, but she ignored him.

Mari settled back in her chair, a faraway look in her eye. "I think it broke his heart when they disbanded the group. He was a dreamer, always thought his ship was about to come in. Oh, don't get me wrong. He was a good worker too. Made a nice living with his crabbing business after that, but he wasn't the same. The spark went out of him when he wasn't on the hunt for treasure."

"I heard about that club." Dom leaned back in his chair and sipped the tea. "It was Benjamin

Hill, Elbert Daniels, Quentin Crane, Billy, and wasn't there a fifth person—a silent partner?"

"Fifth person. Now you know, I'm not sure. My memory gets a bit foggy, and that was long ago. I think I have some photographs, though ..." Mari pushed up from the table eagerly, but then she wobbled and almost fell back. Dom put out a hand to steady her.

"Are you okay?" Claire jumped from her seat to help Mari back into her chair.

Mari waved her off. "I'm fine. Just a dizzy spell. It's nothing. I just need to rest a bit."

"Oh, then perhaps we should leave," Dom said reluctantly. He was eager to see the picture in case the silent partner was in it, but not at the expense of Mari's health. It would just have to wait, and maybe if they gave her some time, she would remember the name of the silent partner.

"Let me help you out to the sofa." Claire grabbed her elbow and steered her toward the living room. "We'll come back tomorrow to finish our visit. Maybe you'll feel better then."

"That's a good idea. I'll dig the brooch out of my jewelry box and try to find those pictures in the basement."

Claire settled Mari on the couch and tucked an orange-and-green crocheted afghan around her legs. "You sure you'll be okay?"

Mari already had the remote control in her hand, and her attention turned to the sixty-inch television in the corner. "I'm perfectly fine. Don't worry. I'll see you two tomorrow."

Dom turned toward the door, his eyebrow tingling. He had a feeling Mari had important information that could be critical to solving the case. Tomorrow could not come soon enough.

Chapter 10

The rain had put a damper on further investigations, so Claire and Dom decided to call it a night after their visit to Mari. Claire had returned to her stone cottage and indulged in a dinner of salmon and sautéed kale and garlic then turned in early, hoping that a good night's rest would jog loose some insights into the case.

But the next day she woke up with just as many questions as the day before.

What had been in the treasure chest to begin with? What kind of evidence was in the storage unit that was so important that someone rushed over to clear it out? And was that person connected to Greenbriar Manor?

And then there was the matter of motive. What was the motive for Elbert's murder in the first place? Was it greed over not wanting to share the treasure, or something else? Because the greed angle didn't pan out if they hadn't found any treasure, as the other members of the treasure-hunting club had been suggesting.

Unless they were lying.

But if they were, and it was greed, why stop at Elbert? There were four people in the treasure club. Wouldn't the greedy person want to kill the others, too, so he could have it all for himself?

What if only one person knew about the treasure? Well, two: the killer and Elbert. Everyone involved claimed no treasure was ever found. Were they all keeping something from Dom and Claire, or did only one of them know that there really was a treasure?

Benjamin and Quentin were the only surviving members. They'd seemed sincere, but Claire had known many other killers who also seemed sincere.

Claire thought about the other treasure club members. Benjamin Hill had protested the digging. He was now quite wealthy, although he claimed it was from investments. Claire made a mental note to investigate his early finances and see if what he claimed was true. Although his grandson, Allen, wasn't so eager for him to talk to them, Benjamin hadn't seemed like he was hiding anything. Maybe Benjamin was a skilled liar and Allen knew more than he was letting on.

Then there was Quentin Crane. He must be quite wealthy to live at Greenbriar Manor. But he'd been happy to talk to them, too, and didn't seem like he was avoiding the subject at all. Then again, he could also be lying.

They couldn't talk to Billy Wilkinson, but Mari certainly didn't live the lavish lifestyle of the widow of someone who had struck it rich, though she did have all the nicer things in her home—new appliances and a big TV.

That left the fifth member. The silent partner. Claire thought of all the wealthy people on the island. Could one of them be the killer? She couldn't think of anyone who had come into money sixty years ago who would also have been the same age to be in the treasure club. There were very few wealthy islanders, but most of them had family money going back much further than sixty years.

Maybe the killer stashed the treasure away to let time pass. Hid it for decades so that it wouldn't be associated with the treasure club. And maybe that person died ... and the treasure was recently discovered. Had someone on the island recently come into money? Someone besides Jane?

Claire had been excited to see Mari's pictures of the treasure-hunting club, but now she realized they wouldn't show the silent partner. None of the other members of the group besides Bill had known who that was, and if he had been in pictures with them, then they would have been able to name him.

Maybe that brooch Mari had would give them something to follow up on. Mari had said the brooch was old and dirty, though. Wouldn't Bill have told her if it was valuable pirate treasure?

Claire pushed away unwanted thoughts of Jane clutching the small box from the storage unit. That box had been small enough to hold several brooches. Claire shook her head. Now she was grasping at straws. There was no way Jane or her father were mixed up in Elbert's death.

Chocolate. Chocolate helped her think better.

Claire went to the kitchen cupboard to search for a piece of dark chocolate. Dark chocolate was her vice. She allowed herself only a few small pieces a day. She hid them around the house so they wouldn't be within easy reach and so she'd have to work to get them.

When her search of the cupboard turned up empty, she moved over to the table beside the overstuffed chair where she did her crossword puzzles. She opened the drawer, sticking her hand way inside to the back. Nope. Nothing there.

There was one last place—the server over by the window. She crossed to the window and pulled open the middle drawer, her hand pushing away the junk-drawer accumulation of papers, keys, and various odd items as she felt for the familiar rectangular shape.

Bingo! She pulled out her hand and smiled at the little rectangle of dark-chocolate ambrosia clutched in her fingers.

The plastic wrapper crinkled, and she popped the candy into her mouth, savoring the sweet, slightly bitter taste. Her gaze drifted out the window. It was dark outside, the sun only a thin orange line at the very edge of the horizon. But something else was lighting the night farther down Israel Head Hill: flashing red and blue lights.

She leaned closer, her face practically touching the cold glass of the window, but she couldn't tell exactly where the light was coming from.

Opening the patio doors, she hurried outside, rushing down to the edge of the property. The storm had cleared out, but the air still had that spring-shower smell, and the ground was soft, especially at the edge of her yard where she now stood, leaning precariously over the railing to try to determine exactly where the lights were coming from.

She leaned out a tad farther and saw Robby's police car parked on the street, the lights flashing and the doors open. Her heart skipped in her chest when she realized where the commotion was.

Mari Wilkinson's house.

Chapter 11

In the pristine kitchen of his condo, Dom lifted the linen napkin from where it sat exactly one inch from the side of his plate. He shook it open and placed it squarely in his lap then turned his attention to the cannoli in the exact middle of his plate.

He picked up the confection and crunched through the outer shell, the creamy, sweet ricotta cheese mixture melting in his mouth. As he chewed, he thought over the case.

So many suspects, but which one was the killer? Had Elbert been killed for the treasure, or was there some other motive? Was the killer even still alive? Who had cleaned out Elbert's storage unit, and who was the woman that had visited it? Did she have a tie-in to the case, or was it coincidence?

"Twiller!" Romeo tweeted as if echoing Dom's thoughts. Dom finished off the cannoli and got a spray of millet from its storage place in the sideboard then opened the cage and clipped it to the side.

Gently petting Romeo's head with his index finger, he said, "You are right, my friend. We need to find the real killer."

Romeo shot a knowing look at him then scurried over to the millet, pecking away at it in quick, sharp movements. Juliet pulled her head from under her wing and cautiously approached the millet spray, pecking at the seeds in a more cautious manner.

"Peepurer," Romeo tweeted.

"Yes. Murderer." Dom's eyes drifted out past the deck, where the orange sun was now kissing the top of the Atlantic. But it wasn't the sun that caught his eye. There seemed to be some sort of a commotion going on down at the bottom of the hill. He couldn't see exactly what it was, but he could see flashing red and blue lights reflecting off the windows of one of the homes.

Dom's eyebrows twitched with the familiar tingle. Something of interest had happened.

He hurried back to the kitchen table, quickly cleaning off his plate and placing it neatly in the dishwasher then making sure to wipe all the crumbs off the table with the small whisk brush he had just for that purpose. Satisfied that his kitchen was in perfect order, he hurried out the door, eager to get to the bottom of the hill and see what, exactly, was going on.

Although Dom routinely walked Israel Head Hill as part of his exercise regimen, he didn't walk this time. He was in too much of a hurry, so he drove, his gut churning as he turned the corner to reveal the source of the commotion was Mari Wilkinson's house. Not surprisingly, Claire was standing right on the front steps.

He hurried to join her, mounting the steps himself just as Robby came out the front door.

"What's happened?" Dom asked in a low voice.

Robby grimaced, leaning in toward Dom and Claire and lowering his voice. "Mari Wilkinson has been murdered. I need some help, Auntie. Can you help hold the crowd back?"

Dom and Claire exchanged a glance. Mari murdered? Surely it was no coincidence. It had to have something to do with Elbert's case.

Even though Robby had kept his voice low, it didn't take long for the truth to circulate. Dom could hear the dismayed whispers as the crowd pressed closer to the house.

Claire turned to face them, holding her palms up. "Stay back, everybody, let the police do their job."

"Do their job? If they were doing their job, a murderer wouldn't be running around loose," someone yelled from the crowd.

"I'm sure they're doing the best they can," Claire shot back.

"Pffft. First old skeletons in treasure chests and now people are being picked off like sitting ducks," Hiram Moody yelled from somewhere in back.

"Yeah, we demand action!" someone else added.

"Now, now," Claire soothed the crowd. "Rob is doing everything he can. I'm sure there is nothing to worry about and the killer will be caught soon. There is no reason to believe that anyone else is in danger. This could be an isolated incident, but if you don't stand back and let him do his job, it will take longer to find who did it."

Zambuco pulled up in his official police car. That's odd, Dom thought, flicking his eyes toward the cove where the ferry was docked. The first run of the day was not for another hour. How in the world did Zambuco get here? He had to be staying somewhere on the island. Dom's eyes slid over to Claire, taking note of the narrow-eyed look she was focusing on Zambuco. Claire must be thinking the same thing and probably coming to the same disturbing conclusion.

If Zambuco was staying somewhere on the island, Dom could only think of one person who would welcome him. Jane.

"Okay, everyone, take it on home." The crowd parted for Zambuco, and he made his way toward Claire and Dom, casting an angry glare at them before turning to address the crowd. "There's nothing to see here. Move it on out."

The crowd started to disperse, and Zambuco turned to Claire and Dom. "That means you, too."

"Of course. We were just trying to help with the crowd," Claire said.

Zambuco snorted and walked into the house.

"Why do they listen to him and not me?" Claire asked, eyeing the dispersing crowd as they headed down the walkway.

"He's meaner." Dom glanced across the street to see Alice James standing on her steps, a pink quilted bathrobe hastily thrown over her pajamas. This was the first time he'd seen her without knitting needles in her hand.

"Look, there's Alice. We should go find out if she saw anything," Dom said.

"Good idea."

Alice tore her eyes from Mari's front door as she noticed them crossing the street, and a smile broke out on her face. "Dom! Claire! What's going on?" She lowered her voice as they came up beside her. "I heard Mari was murdered."

"Afraid so," Dom said.

114

"How terrible." Alice's eyes flicked back over to the crime scene. "Oh, umm... Would you like to come in for some tea?"

Alice's home was a modest cape which appeared not to have been updated since the mid-1970s. The living room boasted a floral sofa and a thick, upholstered La-Z-Boy recliner on top of a large, oval braided rug.

An extra-fluffy orange cat appeared from nowhere and twined itself around Dom's legs.

Claire bent down to pet it. "Hi, Beasley. You just reminded me, I didn't put out any treats for Porch Cat today."

"Oh, Porch Cat came by here earlier this morning. I fed her quite nicely." Alice continued through the open living room doorway into the kitchen and shot over her shoulder, "Is herbal tea okay? I don't have anything stronger."

"Herbal's fine." Dom followed her into the avocado-and-gold kitchen and sat at the glitter-flecked Formica table. Though Alice's furnishings and home were outdated, everything was in pristine condition. It was like stepping into a time machine.

The cat had followed them and sat in front of the refrigerator, swishing her tail and blinking at them, while Alice filled three thick ceramic mugs with hot water and put a basket of tea bags in the middle of the table along with the milk and sugar. Dom picked out an herbal mint, and Claire went with lemon zinger.

Alice sat down and picked up her knitting, winding the purple yarn over the needle, then muttering under her breath and backtracking to rip out stitches.

"Is something upsetting you?" Claire asked.

"There was a murder just next door! Wouldn't you be upset?"

Claire nodded but said nothing.

"I mean, it could have been me!"

"Three out of four murders are committed by someone the victim knows personally," Dom said.

Alice's incredulous look had Dom wondering what he had said wrong. Didn't everyone appreciate statistics as much as he did?

"Everyone knows everyone on this island!" Alice said.

"Only about one out of four murders is committed during some other kind of felony, like robbery. Almost half arise out of arguments. It was probably personal. I'm sure you aren't targeted." Dom settled back in his chair, certain that he had put Alice's fears to rest.

But judging by the way Alice clutched her knitting needles to her chest, it didn't seem as if she was convinced.

Claire rolled her eyes at Dom and placed a soothing hand on Alice's arm. "It's terrible, but don't worry. We'll find who is responsible. For this murder and for Elbert Daniels."

"You think the two are connected?" This thought seemed to calm Alice. Dom reasoned that she figured if Mari's killer had something to do with Elbert, then she had nothing to worry about. He grudgingly admitted that Claire's more touchy-feely methods worked better than statistics to calm people down.

"Almost definitely. We were only talking to Mari yesterday as we followed a lead. Maybe we got too close to the truth," Claire said.

Claire and Dom exchanged a look. Mari had perhaps been going to name the silent partner. Could that person be responsible for both killings?

Claire looked at Alice over the rim of her mug. "Did you see or hear anyone visit Mari last night?"

"No. But then, I had the TV on. I'm getting a little hard of hearing, so I needed to turn it up loud. And it was raining hard last night."

"What about in the past week?" Dom asked. "Has anyone suspicious visited her or lurked around the neighborhood?"

"Suspicious? No. Benjamin Hill and his grandson stopped by, but they do that now and again. Though his grandson didn't seem happy to be carting Ben around like that. A bit ungrateful, if you ask me." Alice pursed her lips and then resumed knitting.

"Anyone else?" Claire asked.

Alice wrinkled her face and looked up at the ceiling. "Well, I saw the Greenbriar Manor shuttle out front in the late afternoon, so maybe Quentin Crane came by. He comes now and again, more infrequently these days. Though, come to think of it, he usually hires a private car. Maybe Mari contacted the manor to see about getting on the waiting list."

All the clues were pointing to the other members of the treasure-hunting club, but Dom couldn't stop thinking about that dirty old brooch Mari had said she had. What if there really was a treasure that only some of the members knew about, and what if those that knew had hidden some of it in plain sight ... like Mari's jewelry box and Elbert's storage unit?

Dom's mind flashed on Marcy telling them about the woman who had come to look at the storage unit. Maybe she was mixed up in this and wanted to claim all the treasure.

"You didn't happen to see a tall, young, brunette woman hanging around, did you?"

"I don't think... Wait, yes! She was driving the Greenbriar shuttle! Why?"

Dom pressed his lips together, not sure what to say. Driving the shuttle? He wasn't expecting that. Surely this was no coincidence, especially in combination with those red pebbles from the meditation garden there.

"Can you think of anyone else who came by? Anyone who might have been out of place?" Claire asked, apparently not as intrigued with the brunette driving the shuttle as Dom.

"No. Well, except...maybe Jane. But she's not out of place. I mean she's an islander, and it's perfectly natural for her to stop by."

"You saw her the other day?" Dom asked.

"Actually, I saw her last night just when the sun went down. Remember the clouds had cleared, and then there was one of those rare downpours where it's raining and the sun is out. I was looking out for a rainbow, and that's when I saw her. She was knocking on Mari's door," Alice said.

Dom exchanged a glance with a green-faced Claire.

"You're sure it was her?" Claire asked. "I mean, you said it was raining, and visibility would have been bad."

"Yes, I'm sure," Alice said. "I'm not blind, you know. I recognized her umbrella right away, you know, the pretty one with those three-dimensional flowers around the edge. But Mari didn't answer her door, so Jane left."

Claire looked relieved, but Dom wasn't so sure. Had Jane really left, or did she gain entry some other way? That was silly. He knew Jane couldn't kill anyone despite the evidence pointing to her.

But would the police see it that way?

Chapter 12

Later that morning, Claire stood in her garden, snapping the branches of one of her rose bushes off violently with her pruning shears. The bush had grown a bit wild over the winter and was blocking the view of the ocean from her favorite bench. She'd been wanting to cut it back and trim it so that the plant was more pleasantly shaped for several weeks now. But she wasn't paying very much attention to what she was doing, her mind on the disturbing discovery of Mari Wilkinson's body.

Alice's confession that she'd seen Jane at Mari's door had disturbed Claire, and she wondered if Dom had noticed how upset she'd been when Alice had mentioned Jane's name. Of course he had. He noticed everything. He was just too considerate to voice what they both knew—a lot of the clues implicated Jane.

But that wasn't the thing that bothered her the most. The thing that bothered her the most was that she'd been so focused on trying to figure out who on the island—besides Jane—could be the killer that she'd overlooked the important clue that a young woman had visited Elbert's locker.

It was no coincidence that the woman had the same description as the one driving the Greenbriar van. But who was this woman, and did she have something to do with Elbert's death? Was she the one who had cleaned out the storage unit? The red pebbles left inside could be a link to Greenbriar after all.

Claire sighed and brushed a gray curl out of her eye with the back of her hand. She stepped back to get a look at her handiwork.

"Darn it all!" The bush looked more like a bonsai experiment gone wrong than the rounded shape she'd been going for. Perhaps now was not the time to be trimming plants.

Claire put down the shears. She was too distracted for this type of meticulous garden work. Instead of tending to her garden, she should be looking into the mysterious brunette. Maybe now that she suspected the mystery woman was connected to Greenbriar, she could make some calls and find out who she was.

She stripped off her gardening gloves and put the hedge clipper away in the toolshed. As she walked across the patio and through the open French doors into the living room, she heard a panicked knocking coming from her door.

"Hold your horses! I'm coming!" Claire rushed over the door. Whoever was on the other side must be desperate to talk to her. Was it Dom? Maybe there had been a breakthrough in the case.

She cracked the door open and looked out at Robby. His hair was a mess, as if he'd been running his hands through it, and his foot tapped nervously on the stoop.

"Robby, what's going on?" Claire asked.

"Can I come in?" He glanced over his shoulder as if expecting someone to come up behind him.

"Of course." Claire opened the door wide, and Robby lurched inside. "Can I get you something to drink? I still have a few of those brownies left over."

"No thanks. I'm good."

Claire studied her nephew. He certainly didn't look good. He looked worried and like he hadn't slept in days. A pang of sympathy shot through her. Having worked in Boston for most of her career, she was used to violent crime. But here on the island, most crimes were nonviolent. With the discovery of Elbert's body and now Mari's murder, Robby might be in over his head.

"Auntie, I know I shouldn't be here, but I need your help."

"What can I help with?"

"Do you think Mari's murder was really connected to Elbert's?"

"It seems that way," Claire said cautiously. She didn't know how much Robby knew of the treasure-hunting club and wasn't sure what information she should share with him. It wasn't Robby so much that she was worried about, but she knew whatever she told him would be used in the investigation and make its way back to Zambuco.

"That's what I was afraid of. I have to admit, I don't know what to do. We've never had a killing spree before. I don't know how to control it." Robby looked almost ready to cry.

"I hardly think you could call two murders spaced sixty years apart a killing spree," Claire pointed out.

Robby scrubbed his hand through his hair, causing it to look even wilder. "You heard the crowd at Mari's earlier. They were ready to attack! If I don't do something, I don't know what will happen."

"Okay, okay. Calm down." Claire led Robby to the sofa, and he sank into the deep cushions. She perched on the edge of the chair across from him. "People can sense when you panic, and it will just cause them to worry, so you have to present a calm front."

"I know, but I'm not sure what to do. That's why I came to you for help. You've seen stuff like this before."

Claire's brows tugged together. "Are you asking me to consult with you officially? Did Zambuco say this was okay?"

"No, but...I don't know what else to do."

Claire chewed her bottom lip. This could be her chance to get some insider information on the case and help her nephew at the same time. She laid her hand on Robby's arm. "It'll be okay. I'm already conducting my own investigation with Dom, if you must know."

"Then you'll help?"

"Of course. But I'll need you to help me so I can help you."

Robby's eyes narrowed. "What do you mean?"

"Dom and I need information to speed up our investigation." Claire sat back in her chair. "I think we might be able to help you catch your killer if we could have one hour uninterrupted in Mari Wilkinson's house."

"Oh, I don't know if Zambuco would let—"

"He doesn't need to know. But we do need to get in there if you want us to help you."

"Okay, well, I guess I could arrange that," Robby said hesitantly.

"And we'll need to know everything you know about the murder case so far, including when Mari died."

"I don't know much right now. The techs just got done going through the house for DNA and fingerprint evidence. We didn't find the murder weapon in the house. It appears as though she was bludgeoned to death. The ME estimates time of death between seven and eight last night."

Dread bloomed in Claire's chest as she digested Robby's words. When had Alice seen the Greenbriar shuttle? Claire didn't think she'd mentioned a specific time, but she remembered her saying it was late afternoon. There was a big stretch between late afternoon and around seven in the evening. The sun set at half past seven, so surely Alice wouldn't call that late afternoon. But Alice had made reference to someone she'd seen there right after the sun had set.

That person was Jane.

Chapter 13

Mari Wilkinson's house still looked the same as it had when she and Dom had visited the day before, but to Claire, it seemed much sadder and emptier today.

After Robby had agreed to let them into the house, she hadn't wasted a second. She'd called Dom, and the three of them headed over right away. She didn't want to give Robby any time to change his mind.

Robby didn't want anyone to see them going in, so he'd driven his car to Mari's and parked out front as if on official police business, while Claire and Dom walked down from Claire's, cutting through the neighbor's backyard and approaching the house from the back. Robby lifted the yellow crime scene tape that was strung around the small back porch, and Claire ducked under.

Robby leveled her a look as he opened the kitchen door for them. "Don't disturb anything."

"We've done this a time or two before, you know," Claire said.

"I know." Robby glanced around as if to reassure himself that they hadn't been spotted. "You have an hour, maybe less. I'll keep watch."

Dom and Claire hurried inside without speaking. They'd decided their plan of attack on the phone earlier. Dom was to inspect the crime scene—Mari's living room—and Claire was to look for the brooch and pictures Mari had mentioned earlier.

Inside, Dom walked straight to the living room, and Claire headed down the hall. She didn't know which bedroom was Mari's, but she figured it wouldn't take Sherlock Holmes to figure that out. She expected to find the queen-size bed and old pine dressers. What she didn't expect was the chaos that surrounded them.

The entire room was thrown askew. Drawers pulled out and clothes on the floor. The jewelry box was dumped on the bed, its contents spilled all over the colorful quilt.

Did the killer do this, or was Mari just a messy housekeeper?

The rest of the house was neatly kept. It must have been the killer unless Mari was one of those that was neat in the public living areas and messy in private.

Claire took a deep breath and entered the room. There was something about going through the belongings of the dead that creeped her out, but she needed to look for the brooch and the photos. She pulled her lime-green gardening gloves out of her pocket. Though she didn't think leaving her fingerprints would be a problem, it was an old habit from her crime scene investigating days.

Approaching the bed, she bent over to survey the mess. It was a jumble of jewelry, mostly newer, none of it particularly valuable. She moved the pieces around carefully with her index finger but did not find an old, dirty brooch.

She turned her attention to the rest of the room. She inspected the drawers, the closet, she even looked in the small drawer of the nightstand, but no old photos or brooches were to be found.

Had the killer taken the photos, too? Or had Mari never gotten the chance to dredge them up from the basement?

Claire went back to the living room to find Dom rubbing his eyebrow and staring at Mari's chair.

He turned to her. "Anything?"

"I didn't find a brooch, but someone searched Mari's room. It's a mess in there."

Dom's brows shot up. He stepped past her down the hall to see for himself. He moved to the middle of the room and quietly looked over the mess. Claire tried not to feel put out. She'd already searched in there. Did he think he could find something she hadn't? Then again, he often did.

"A hasty search. They didn't have much time, it seems," Dom said. "Or they found what they came for quickly."

"The brooch," Claire said. "So Mari's murder does tie into the treasure."

"It would seem that way, unless the brooch wasn't in her jewelry box, and the killer was looking for something else."

"Or Mari kept a really messy bedroom," Claire said. "What do you make of the crime scene?"

"Come and I'll show you."

Claire bit back a sarcastic remark as Dom led the way to the living room. He loved showing off his theories with detailed—and sometimes boring —explanations. It wasn't that Claire didn't want to learn more about interpreting the physical clues, it was just that sometimes it seemed like Dom was a tad bit full of himself.

Dom pointed to the wall behind the chair, which was dotted with a spray of blood.

"The pattern suggests that whatever Mari was struck with was wielded from above the head, probably by someone who was on the tall side. But the blows were not dealt too forcefully." Dom raised his clasped hands just above his head and brought them down, mimicking the action. "Mari was older and a bit frail. She likely could not fight them off. But the fact that she was sitting in the chair indicates that she had invited them into her home."

"So she knew her killer." Claire said it as a statement.

"It would seem so."

"And the killer was tall?" Claire asked. Most of their suspects were tall. But not Jane. "Would Benjamin or Quentin have the strength to bludgeon her?"

Dom pinched his chin. "I think so. They are elderly men, but Benjamin exhibited much vigor in his protest of the digging, and Quentin seemed rather fit. It wouldn't take much force."

She hated to think that one of the islanders, especially Bill or Quentin, who knew Mari, would kill her in such a violent manner. Her thoughts turned to the young woman who had been seen at the storage unit and here at Mari's house.

But that couldn't be right. Claire knew in her gut that Elbert's murder and Mari's murder were connected, and they both had something to do with the treasure. The woman who kept cropping up in the investigation was too young to have killed Elbert.

"Ten more minutes," Robbie yelled in the door, spurring Claire and Dom into action.

"You didn't find the photographs Mari mentioned?" Dom asked.

"No. Either the killer took them or they're still down in the basement." Claire opened the basement door and gestured for Dom to precede her.

The two of them climbed down the rickety wooden stairs, the smell of mold growing stronger as they descended. "It's damp down here. I hope these old pictures haven't been destroyed by mildew."

"Hopefully, if they are here, we'll still be able to make out what is in them." Dom stood in the middle of the basement. Boxes were piled up around all the walls. "Where do we start?"

"The pictures would've been from sixty years ago, so we should start towards the back. That's where the older things would be stored." Claire felt a perverse pleasure that this time she was instructing Dom as to what to do. She picked her way to the far wall, shoving boxes out of her path as she went.

She rummaged quickly, opening the tops of the boxes and peering inside. Kitchenware. Old linens. Boxes of decades-old baby toys. Finally, she opened a box to find stacks of loose photos.

"In here!"

Dom came over to join her, and they sorted through the box, picking up handfuls of photos and flipping through quickly.

"Look!"

Dom held a pile of old Polaroids. The pictures were yellowed with age, the colors melded into muted shades of sepia, but you could clearly make out the subject matter.

One showed younger versions of Bill, Quentin, Elbert, and Benjamin proudly holding metal detectors. Another showed Bill and Quentin digging something out of the ground. In the third picture, a smiling Elbert held up an old coin.

But it was the fourth picture that caught their interest. This picture showed the interior of the storage unit with a man inside. Not Bill, Elbert, Quentin, or Benjamin. It looked like he was inspecting the equipment. In his right hand, he held a clipboard.

Claire's stomach swooped.

"That could be the silent partner. Turn it over. Maybe his name is written on the back," Dom said.

"I don't need to. That's Charlie Kuhn, Jane's father."

***

Dom thought about the picture as they made their way back up the stairs. It was just a picture, certainly not proof that Charlie Kuhn was the silent partner. But Dom's gut told him that Charlie was the fifth member. It was evident by the way the man was clearly inventorying the equipment in the photo. And judging by the tight look on Claire's face, she had come to the same conclusion.

That didn't mean that Charlie was the killer or that Jane was running around town taking steps to cover that fact up. Did it?

Jane had recently come into money. Jane had been seen at Mari's door last night right around the time she was killed. Jane visited Greenbriar frequently and probably took her mother to the meditation garden, and Jane was seen at the storage facility.

Even with these clues pointing to Jane, Dom didn't believe she was a killer. Dom didn't have the skills to analyze behavior like Claire did, but he was pretty good at reading people. He'd put dozens of killers behind bars, and he knew Jane was no killer. He'd stake his reputation on it.

Which meant they had to find the real killer before the police added up the clues and started looking at Jane.

Robby was waiting for them outside the kitchen door with a hopeful expression on his face. "Did you find anything?"

"No," Claire said.

Dom slid his eyes over to her and added, "Nothing that you probably don't already know. We think the killer must be tall or have wielded a weapon easy to lift above their head."

Robby nodded. "That's what I thought and the ME verified."

"Sorry we weren't more help," Dom said. "We'll keep investigating though. Will you keep us apprised of any developments?"

"Sure." Robby turned concerned eyes on Claire. "Auntie, are you okay? You're awfully quiet."

"What?" Claire looked at Robby then back at the house. "Oh, I'm fine. Must be getting a cold."

"Do you need a ride back?" Robby asked.

"No." Dom grabbed Claire's elbow and led her away. "We need the exercise."

"Okay." Robby's face registered sheer disappointment as he locked the door. "You'll let me know what you come up with?"

"Of course." Once they were out of earshot, Dom turned to Claire. "I have coffee at my place. We need to talk."

Claire nodded, and they walked the rest of the way in silence, each preoccupied with their own thoughts. When they got to his condo, Dom ushered Claire into the kitchen and sat her at the table while he made coffee.

"Sorry I don't have any tea," he said over his shoulder as he filled black ceramic mugs with the brew.

"That's fine. I could use something stronger."

Romeo sidestepped his way along his perch to the side of his cage, peering out at Dom as he put the mugs on the table.

"Twuspect."

"Yes, my friend, we have a suspect. Several, in fact." Dom sat, cupping his hands around the mug. "But still, I'm not sure which one is most likely to be the culprit."

Claire looked over at him. "And is Jane one of your suspects?"

Dom shrugged. "Jane or her father. Of course, he couldn't have killed Mari."

Claire's eyes widened. "You can't believe that Jane could do something like that!"

"You know I rely on evidence, not feelings. I go wherever the evidence leads me."

"Even if the evidence is wrong?"

"Let's think about this rationally. If that picture was of someone other than Jane's father, we would be talking to them next."

"But we already spoke to her about Elbert's murder."

"And she admitted that her dad knew Elbert and Bill Wilkinson. They were friends even. They came to her house."

"True, but that doesn't mean much. Most everyone on the island knows each other."

"Jane said her dad talked to Bill about collections. Let me pose a scenario to you—"

"You don't pose scenarios. You find evidence," Claire said weakly.

"Just listen to me. Mari Wilkinson had that brooch, right?"

Claire nodded.

"What if that brooch was only part of what was in the treasure chest, and Bill and Charlie split the rest?"

"What about the rest of them?" Claire asked, then her eyes narrowed. "Surely you don't mean that they cut the others out of the treasure ... and killed Elbert!"

"Not necessarily, but—"

"Jane's father didn't have any money. If he'd had a big treasure, then why have Jane and her mom struggled financially their whole lives ..."

"Until recently." Dom finished her thought.

"You've noticed Jane's had more money lately, too," Claire said quietly.

"I've noticed. The car. The necklace. Her mom's in an expensive facility. She seems less worried when we eat out."

"But if her dad dug up that treasure, wouldn't she have been rich before?"

"Maybe she just found the money. Maybe he hid it. Maybe that's why she was in the storage unit."

Claire sipped her coffee thoughtfully. "No, that doesn't make sense. And what about the other members of the club? They insisted that they never found anything."

"Clearly one of them lied, or else the other two were somehow cut out of the deal. Just like Elbert was."

"Except not in such a drastic manner, as they are both still living."

"Look, I don't think Jane killed Mari any more than you do. But what if she suspected her father killed Elbert and was trying to cover for him? She might have needed that brooch in order to do it. Mari was possibly the only living person who could have told us that the silent partner was Charlie."

"I know that...but she wouldn't. I mean, he's dead. What does it matter now even if he was the killer?"

"Would you like for the island to discover that your father was a murderer?"

"Good point."

"Alice saw Jane at Mari's the night of the murder, remember? And Robby told me that time of death was very soon after that." Claire's face paled. "If the police come to the same conclusions we just did, they might not think so leniently of Jane."

"Exactly." Dom leveled his gaze at Claire. "Do you think Zambuco would arrest her, though?"

Claire's brow ticked up. "Oh, you noticed they seem to be awfully ... umm ... friendly too?"

Dom nodded.

Claire shuddered. "I'm not sure if he would let whatever he has going on with her cloud his judgment. Maybe. And if he did, that would be even worse because he might be inclined to prosecute an innocent person in his haste to deflect attention from Jane."

"All the more reason for us to find the truth. We have other suspects, and I'm not so sure Jane's father was involved in Elbert's killing."

"I'd hate to think he was. He was a gentle man, and it would kill Jane if her father was a murderer." Claire sighed. "Unfortunately, anything he might be able to tell us about the treasure-hunting club and what happened sixty years ago is buried with him."

Dom stroked his chin. "Yes, that is a shame, but everything he knew might not necessarily be lost."

"What do you mean?"

A pang of sadness pierced Dom's heart. "There's a person that one tends to share everything with ... at least I did before ..."

"Your spouse." Claire shot up from the table. "We need to talk to Jane's mother."

Chapter 14

Claire and Dom were lucky enough to catch the early-afternoon ferry to the mainland. It was a clear, sunny day, but Claire didn't take any joy in the warmth of the sun on her shoulders or the salty sea breeze on her cheeks—she was too impatient to get to Greenbriar Manor and some information that would shed light on the case.

Preferably light that pointed away from Jane and her father.

As they drove up the drive to the manor, guilt washed over her. She felt as if she was going behind Jane's back, but she didn't want to ask Jane for fear her friend might not understand that Claire needed the information to prove her innocence and not because she suspected her of any wrongdoing. She wouldn't broach the subject with Jane unless it was absolutely necessary.

On their way into the building, Claire noticed an aide wheeling someone along the path beside the manor.

"I think that's Lila over there." Claire tilted her head toward the wheelchair.

Dom glanced over. "So it is."

They veered off in that direction just as the nurse was parking Lila next to a rose bush laden with velvety red buds, some of which were already unfurling. The enormous, thorny bush climbed a trellis attached to the side of the building and reached almost to the second floor. Claire eyed it with appreciation, wondering if her rose bush would someday grow as large.

"Hello." The aide greeted them pleasantly. "Are you here to see Lila?"

"Yes. I'm Claire Watkins, a friend of Lila's daughter Jane," Claire said.

"Wonderful. I'll leave you here to visit while I run inside." She maneuvered the wheelchair so that the back was against the wall of the building, giving Lila a view of the garden. She patted Lila's hand as she bent down to lock the wheels. "I'll leave you to visit with your friends. I'll be back in ten minutes."

The aide shot a smile at Claire and Dom over her shoulder as she headed toward the front door.

Lila watched her walk away then cast a hazy look at both Claire and Don. "Do I know you?"

"Yes, Mrs. Kuhn. It's me, Claire." Claire bent down to kiss Lila's cheek and took a seat on the bench beside her.

Lila smiled at Claire then eyed Dom suspiciously.

"This is my friend Dominic Benedetti," Claire said.

Lila nodded, seemingly satisfied with the introductions, and closed her eyes, taking a deep breath. "I love the sun on my face and the smell of the roses. You know you can smell the sea from here?"

"Yes. It's lovely." Claire had to admit the sun did feel good, and the fragrant floral scent mixed with fresh-mowed grass and the briny smell of the sea was invigorating.

"So peaceful here." No sooner did the words escape Lila's lips than a clatter sounded from the open window next to them.

"Well, except that. That's the south sitting room, I believe. Noise travels right out to this very spot." Lila's lucid remarks gave Claire hope. Maybe they would be able to get something good out of her.

"Mrs. Kuhn, we were wondering if we could ask you some questions," Claire said.

Lila opened her eyes and looked at Claire. "Who did you say you were?"

Okay, maybe she wasn't quite so lucid. "Claire. Claire Watkins. I'm a friend of Jane's."

"Janey? Janey isn't friends with any senior citizens, or I would know about it."

Claire exchanged a troubled look with Don, but she pressed on. "We wanted to ask you some questions about your husband Charlie."

Lila sighed, a smile flitting across her lips. "I wish that Charlie was back. He's always away on his trips."

Claire couldn't remember Jane's dad taking many trips, but it was an awfully long time ago, and her memory was admittedly fuzzy on the matter. In fact, she could barely picture Jane's dad at all. Still, she had to wonder if any of Lila's answers would be real memories or manufactured ones.

"We heard that he was part of a treasure-hunting club," Dom said.

Lila's voice grew soft, her eyes clouded with old memories. "Oh yes... but if you want in, they aren't accepting any new members. It's just the four of them. And Charlie, of course, but he doesn't do any of the hunting."

"So you knew about it?" Dom asked.

"Of course. A good husband always tells his wife everything. He believes in that silly superstition that William Kidd buried treasure here. A waste of money, if you ask me." Her face turned sour. "That Billy Wilkinson is a bad influence on Charlie."

More sounds drifted out of the window, making it difficult to hear Lila, as her voice was so low. Claire scooted forward in her seat to get closer to Lila.

"Bill and Charlie are friends?" Claire asked.

"Best friends. It's Billy who convinced Charlie to go in with him on this treasure-hunting thing. What about our Janey, I ask you? She needs to go to college."

More sounds drifted out of the window. A familiar voice caught her attention, and Claire cocked an ear toward the window.

"Mr. Crane, can you tell me why I just got a phone call from your doctor telling me that you never made your appointment yesterday? You have to stop skipping those appointments. I saw you get into the private car, and you need that therapy if you want your knees to stay strong," a stern voice said.

"I didn't feel like going."

Was that Quentin Crane? It sounded like him, though his voice was rougher and more crotchety than the other day.

"You were out all afternoon. Where were you?" the stern voice asked.

"I didn't know this was a prison. Is a man not allowed to take a walk along the water anymore?" Quentin said.

"I'm just here to help. If you're having troubles with your memory or if you're feeling bad, I need to know about it so I can address it in your treatment plan."

"I'm fine. Did you reschedule with the doctor? I promise to go next time ..."

Quentin's voice faded away, and a sound from Lila brought Claire's attention back to her.

"Now that Quentin Crane, I like him much better than Bill," Lila said.

"Quentin is friends with Charlie too?" Claire asked.

Lila nodded. "He was in the club. A very nice man. In fact, I had him over for tea just the other day."

"Oh really?" Claire and Dom exchanged a glance.

Lila nodded. "Yes. The roses were in full bloom, and he picked a bouquet to take back to his wife. Such a thoughtful young man."

Claire glanced at the rose bush. It wasn't in full bloom. Lila must be remembering something from her past.

Lila's eyes clouded. "He said my Charlie is waiting behind the golden doors."

"Did Bill or Charlie ever show Quentin the brooch?"

Lila narrowed her eyes at Dom.

"Brooch. No! You can take it back. We don't want it. I won't show it to Charlie!" Lila's voice rose. She was clearly upset ... and clearly not lucid.

"It's okay. It's fine. We'll take it back," Claire tried to soothe her.

"He's spending a fortune on your stupid treasure-hunting business, Elbert. I don't care how many brooches you found in that chest. We don't want those worthless pieces of crap," Lila sobbed, flinging her hands out at Dom.

An aide hurried around the corner, her brows furrowed at Claire and Dom upon seeing Lila's agitation. She hurried over to the wheelchair. "Now, Mrs. Kuhn, calm down." She rubbed Lila's shoulders and made clucking noises until Lila relaxed.

"Oh, okay, is lunch ready?" Lila asked.

"Lunch was an hour ago, but we can get you a snack." The aide glanced at Claire and Dom again. "I think it's time you went inside anyway."

"Yes, I'm tired now, but it's been lovely talking to Gertrude and Harold." Lila nodded at Claire and Dom, and the nurse unlocked the wheelchair and wheeled her away, leaving them sitting in the garden alone.

"Well, that wasn't exactly what I expected," Dom said.

"Me either, but can we really trust her memory?" Claire asked. "I don't remember Charlie traveling a lot, so if she was mistaken about that ..."

"She could have been mistaken about everything else she said. But she mentioned an old brooch, and it would be too much of a coincidence that she would randomly make that up. She must've seen a brooch back in the treasure-hunting days, but she might be confused about the circumstances."

"Which means they did find treasure in that chest, and Charlie and Bill knew about it."

"And Elbert ... and who knows who else. The others could very well be lying."

Claire's shoulders slumped. "We're no closer to the truth than we were earlier."

"Maybe, maybe not. I don't think we can take Lila's memories as gospel, but it gives us a little more to go on. Charlie likely knew about the brooch and possibly anything else that was in the chest."

"There's one other thing," Claire said as they started toward the car. "I overheard that conversation from the window, and it sounded like Quentin Crane might be a little senile himself. Maybe we can't trust his memories, either."

"Really? Why?"

"The nurse said he'd missed his doctor's appointment. Said she was worried about his memory."

"Hmm. Well, he didn't really tell us much of anything to begin with, so that's no great loss. Maybe he really doesn't remember finding any treasure. There's one thing about this that worries me, though."

"Oh?"

"If Elbert was the one to find the brooch, why did Mari Wilkinson claim her husband had found it? And if Elbert brought it to Charlie, maybe Charlie had something to do with Elbert's death after all."

Chapter 15

Claire had no choice but to go and talk to Jane. She couldn't rely on Lila's faulty memory, and she needed to get to the bottom of this. For Jane's sake. She just hoped that saving Jane from becoming the number-one suspect in a murder investigation wouldn't ruin their friendship.

Butterflies swamped her stomach as she approached Jane's door. Memories of them as young girls and teenagers surfaced. Happy memories. And then the sad ones when Jane's father died. She remembered how devastated both Jane and her mom had been. Her heart crunched, hoping the results of her investigation wouldn't have to mar the memory of Charlie Kuhn.

Claire hadn't taken a good look at the house in a while. Jane had lived in a townhouse a few streets over, and her mom had stayed in this house, the one Jane had grown up in, until recently. It was an older house on a big lot. Claire noticed the yard had become overgrown. The farthest section overlooking Smugglers' Cove was practically a jungle. She noticed the house also looked a bit run-down. She also noticed that

Shane McDonough's truck was in the driveway. Now that Jane was living in the house, she must be having him tend to the necessary repairs.

Claire raised her fist to knock, hoping that she wasn't intruding. She hadn't called Jane ahead of time and hated just popping in unannounced. But she needed answers, so hopefully Jane wasn't busy doing something. And hopefully that something didn't involve Zambuco.

"Claire! What a pleasant surprise. Come on in." Jane held the door wide, and Claire stepped inside, looking tentatively for signs of Zambuco. She didn't see any sign of him, thankfully, but what she did see was a pile of boards. Which explained the hammering sounds that were coming from the kitchen.

"Are you renovating the kitchen?" Claire asked.

"It's long overdue, don't you think? Mom never had it redone, so it's almost seventy years old."

"Well, I suppose it is." Claire peeked into the kitchen on her way through to the living room. Shane McDonough was bent over his table saw, pencil in hand. He glanced up and smiled at Claire. She smiled back in return, taking in the extensive renovation in progress. This was no small spruce-up. The cabinets were down.

Flooring ripped up and appliances gone. Her heart sank. Where had Jane gotten the money for such an expensive renovation?

"Have a seat." Jane pointed to the sofa, and Claire sat.

"I'm afraid I can't offer you any tea or coffee. The stove's been pulled out for the renovation," Jane said.

"That's fine. I just wanted to come and visit. Seems like we've both been so busy we haven't had time to catch up." Guilt shot through Claire. It was true they hadn't talked in a while, but the real reason she was here wasn't to catch up. She needed information from Jane about her father's involvement in the treasure club and to find out why she had been at Mari's. Now, how to approach the subject?

"I have been busy with the renovations and ... well, you've probably been busy with your investigation, right?" Jane said eagerly. Almost too eagerly. Was she fishing for information? No matter. She'd opened the conversation to the very topic Claire wanted to discuss, and Claire wasn't one to look a gift horse in the mouth.

"Yes, it has kept me quite busy," Claire said. "And now with what's happened to Mari ..."

Jane leaned forward. "Do you think that has something to do with Elbert's murder?"

"Maybe. The murders were sixty years apart, so it's hard to say." Claire settled back on the sofa and studied Jane. "I was wondering, though, if you might have some information about Mari."

"Me? What kind of information would I have?"

"Alice said she saw you at Mari's the night of the murder."

"Clearly Alice's eyesight is getting worse. I was here that night. Just ask—"

Claire waited for Jane to say more, but after a few seconds when she didn't, Claire asked, "Just ask who?"

Jane's cheeks turned crimson. "No one. I was here all night, though."

Claire didn't want to ask who Jane had been about to refer to. Was it Zambuco? That would certainly be an airtight alibi. She could tell by the way Jane was fidgeting and her stiff body posture that she was hiding something, but was she hiding the fact that she'd lied about not being at Mary's or merely nervous because she didn't want Claire to know Zambuco had been at her house that night?

But if Jane really had been here at home, then who had Alice seen at Mari's door?

Not wanting to press Jane on that further, Claire decided to change subjects. "Did you know that your dad was a part of the same treasure-hunting club that Elbert was in?"

Jane's eyes widened in surprise. Apparently she hadn't known about the treasure-hunting club ... or she was surprised that Claire had found out about it.

"You know I don't remember much about my dad." Jane's wistful eyes drifted to the window. "I was so young when he died. And you know how teens are so self-absorbed. I'm afraid I never really paid much attention to what was going on in his life."

Jane's phone blared a staccato buzz ringtone, and she glanced down at the table to see the caller ID display. "Oh, it's Greenbriar Manor. This could be about my mom. I need to take it."

"Of course," Claire said.

Jane picked up the phone and answered, walking down the hall to take the call in private. The work noises in the kitchen stopped, and Shane poked his head into the room, wiping his hands on a red cloth.

"Hey, Claire, how's it going?" he asked.

"Very well, thanks. How's the work coming?"

"Great. Jane's kept me busy over the winter, what with finishing the basement and redoing the bathroom."

Claire's brows tugged together. "She has?"

"Yes. In fact, I'm going to admire my handiwork now." Shane smiled and turned toward the bathroom.

Claire chewed on her bottom lip. The renovations were more extensive than she even imagined. She knew a good kitchen renovation could cost tens of thousands, and a bathroom couldn't be far behind. Jane didn't have the money to afford this ... at least she didn't used to have the money.

But Claire was convinced there must be some other explanation for her friend coming into money. It didn't make any sense that it was related to the treasure club of sixty years ago. Why would it just be showing up now? Maybe Jane had taken a second mortgage on the house. Her parents had lived here for long enough that it was certainly paid off by now.

Claire glanced around the room. Were there any new expensive items? No. The sofa was the old one from Jane's townhouse, and everything else looked to be either Jane's or left over from her parents.

Her eye fell on a box stuffed behind the armchair on the other side of the room, a cardboard box just like the one Jane had been holding at the storage facility.

Unable to stop herself, Claire scurried over to the box and flipped open the top with her index finger, steeling herself for what she might find inside. She relaxed when she saw there were no old brooches in the box as she had feared. What was in there was paperwork. An old passport, plane ticket stubs, and a journal or ledger of some sort, written in a handwriting that was not Jane's. The front read Property of Charlie Kuhn.

Could this be Charlie's inventory of the metal-detecting equipment? And if it was, would it give them any clues? She couldn't take the journal. That would be like stealing from Jane.

Claire leaned back to peer down the hall. Jane was still on the phone, her back turned, her head bowed. Claire whipped out her cell phone. Flipping through the pages quickly, she took as many pictures as she dared. Then she stuffed the ledger back into the box and hurried back to her spot on the sofa.

Jane returned to the room. "Sorry that took so long. Apparently Mom was upset by some visitors today, and they wanted to know if they could give her a sedative."

Claire felt a new wave of guilt. Were she and Dom the visitors that had upset Lila? "Oh, that's terrible. I hope your mom is okay."

"Yes, she's fine now, thanks. So anyway, what have you been up to? I mean besides the investigation."

Claire's eyes slid over to the box behind the sofa. She didn't want to sit around making small talk now that she had this extra evidence to investigate.

"Oh, not much. You know, experimenting with my healthy dessert recipes and all." Claire looked at her watch. "Will you look at the time? I guess I better be going."

Jane's face registered surprise. "Oh, so soon?"

"Sorry. I promised Robby I'd make him an apple pie, and I have to get started."

Claire cringed at the look of disappointment on Jane's face. She felt like a heel for lying to her but consoled herself with the fact that it was all to help her.

"Well, it was nice to see you." Jane rose and walked Claire to the door. "Let me know if you find anything more on Elbert's case ... or Mari's."

"Right. Will do." Claire hustled off, hoping that letting Jane know about her progress in the case wouldn't involve telling her that her father had been a cold-blooded killer.

Chapter 16

On the way to Dom's, Claire almost drove off the road because she was so busy looking at the pictures of the journal she'd taken on her phone. She peeled into the parking space across from his condo and rushed up his walk, unsurprised at the look of concern that bloomed on his face when he opened the door. She was sure she looked as frazzled as she felt.

"What's happened?" Dom asked.

Claire thrust her phone out toward him. "I found a box at Jane's. The box she had in the storage unit. There was an old journal inside. I took these pictures."

Dom grabbed her elbow and pulled her inside, leading her to the living room and pushing her into an oversized chair. "What was in it?"

"I'm not sure, but I think it looks like an inventory of some sort. The journal was old, the ink faded to a light blue." Claire bit her bottom lip. "I'm afraid it's the journal Charlie used for the detecting equipment, and it might hold information that could give us some insight as to what, exactly, they found in that treasure chest. There's some entries in the back that look to be coded, and I don't know how to decipher them."

"Let me take a look. I'll have to get my glasses." Dom went into the attached dining room and rummaged in the sideboard, pulling out a small pair of half-moon glasses, which he perched on his nose.

"Tuclueee," Romeo tweeted happily in his cage.

"Yes, hopefully there is a clue," Dom said as he returned to the living room. He sat on the couch opposite Claire and concentrated on the pictures, using his index finger to scroll through slowly.

Claire took the time to notice her surroundings. Though she'd been in his kitchen many times, this was the first time she'd actually sat in Dom's living room. She was surprised to find it was tastefully furnished with contemporary furniture in a muted gray microfiber. The coffee and end tables were a black-stained wood, the carpet a medium gray, the walls a lighter tone. The pillows on the couch were arranged perfectly, a fact that did not surprise Claire given Dom's compulsion to have everything in perfect order.

On the couch, Dom was now using his finger and thumb to zoom in on the photos. Claire studied his face as he flipped from photo to photo,

161

his brow furrowing deeper with each passing second. Finally he set the phone down and fixed Claire with a serious look.

"I'm afraid this leaves little doubt that Charlie Kuhn was the silent partner of the treasure-hunting club," he said.

"It says that?"

"Not in so many words, but there are figures in some of the early pages pertaining to the cost of equipment and repair to said equipment."

"That's all?" Claire relaxed into the chair. "That's a relief. All that indicates is that Charlie Kuhn was the silent partner. Nothing in there proves that he stole treasure or killed Elbert."

"True, but there is something here that makes him suspicious. Toward the end, it's hard to make out, but there is the name and address of a high-profile collector and antique dealer on the mainland. Then there are expenses listed for a trip, presumably to see the collector."

"Then they did find something of value."

Dom nodded. "Judging by the figures scrawled on the next page, they found a lot of something. The figures are listed next to serial numbers."

"Serial numbers?"

"I can't be sure without verifying, but they look like treasury bonds to me."

"Wait. Bonds? That explains it! Charlie didn't have a lot of money sixty years ago because those bonds could've taken thirty years to mature." Claire pressed her lips together. "But they would have matured decades ago, so why is Jane just coming into money now?"

"When did Charlie pass away?"

"Oh gosh, it must've been fifty years or more ..." Claire let her voice trail off as an idea niggled its way to the front of her brain. "What if he never told Jane or her mom about the treasure or the bonds? He may have hidden the bonds away, thinking he would cash them in thirty years later so as not to be associated with the treasure. But he died before he could cash them in. Jane and Lila may have never known he had them."

Dom nodded slowly. "That would make sense. Jane came into the money shortly before she put her mother in Greenbriar. Her mother was already failing then, and Jane was probably starting to clean out the house, go through old things. She might have come across the bonds then."

"But if this theory is true, it proves that someone was lying about finding treasure," Claire said.

"And that Charlie knew about it," Dom added.

"Maybe the treasury bonds were bought with some of the treasure money. It will be good to know how much those were worth. Can we look at the serial numbers?"

"I suppose we could, but do we really need to? It's evident that Jane has a large sum of extra money. The only question is, did Jane know that money came from the treasure-hunting club and, if she did, did she suspect her father's involvement in Elbert's death ... and if so, did she take measures to keep that quiet by silencing Mari?"

Claire's spirits sank. Dom had a point. "But none of this proves that Charlie had anything to do with Elbert's death."

"True, but if our theory holds true, then Charlie was hiding the fact that he had come into a lot of money. Why would he hide that?"

"So you think he could've found the treasure, possibly with Elbert, and the two of them decided to cut the others out, and then Charlie killed Elbert to have it all to himself."

"Either that or they're all lying about finding treasure. But they really would have no reason to lie unless they wanted to hide something like Elbert's death." Dom glanced down at the phone again. "All we can tell from here for sure is that Charlie brought something to the antique dealer over on the mainland. Whatever it was presumably came from the treasure chest. He knew about the treasure."

"And the others claimed there was no treasure."

"So either they're lying, or Charlie had something to hide."

Claire shook her head. "I refuse to believe Charlie had anything to do with Elbert's death. He was a gentle man. A good man."

"Money makes people do funny things."

"This is all theory. We need concrete evidence. We need to take it to the next level and find out more about what the police know. Robby asked for our help and said he'd share information with us, and I think it's time I give him a call and have him make good on that promise."

Claire snatched her phone off the table just as a knock sounded on the door. Fingers poised above the phone screen, she leaned over the arm of her chair to see who it was.

The side window that ran the length of Dom's front door didn't show much. All she could see was a large, bulky figure shuffling from one foot to another. "My word, is that Zambuco?"

"Well, you did want to talk to the police..." Dom let his voice trail off as he got up to answer the door.

"Detective Zambuco, what a pleasant surprise. Do come in." Claire wondered if Zambuco noticed the sarcastic undertone in Dom's voice.

Zambuco tripped over the threshold and stumbled into the living room, his eyes narrowing as he noticed Claire. "Fancy seeing you here. You two wouldn't happen to be investigating the recent murder, would you?"

"We're retired, remember?" Dom gestured for him to take a seat in the other chair.

"You and I both know that doesn't stop you." Zambuco sat stiffly, and the room fell silent except for the soft tap-tap-tap of Zambuco's fingers drumming on the arm of the chair.

Claire wondered what, exactly, it was that he wanted, but she didn't speak. She knew it would give her and Dom a psychological advantage to wait it out and let Zambuco speak first. She suppressed a smile when she realized Dom was doing the same. She'd taught him well.

"I need your help." Zambuco's voice was soft, pleading instead of his usual gruff, abrasive tone.

Claire exchanged a stunned glance with Dom. She'd assumed that Zambuco had discovered that Robby had let them into Mari's house and was expecting him to read them the riot act. Instead he was here asking for their help. He'd never done that before. Things must be drastically wrong.

"You're asking us for help? After you warned us away from the case?" Claire asked.

"Yes."

"Why?" Dom asked.

Zambuco's face contorted into a painful-looking grimace. Part of Claire felt sorry for him. The other part found perverse enjoyment in the fact that he was obviously conflicted and in some sort of emotional pain.

"Come on, you guys have been looking into this case. You must have discovered the same things I have. Things are pointing toward Jane's father and possibly even Jane," Zambuco said. "I know Jane would never do anything wrong, but as an officer of the law, I can't ignore the clues. I have to put the case together based on those. My hands are tied because I can't go outside the law to find the real truth. And furthermore, the brass is breathing down my neck. They want the suspect in custody today."

Claire studied Zambuco. He looked genuinely distraught over the thought of implicating Jane. "You really care for her, don't you?"

"Of course I do."

Claire hadn't been a fan of Jane getting involved with Zambuco. Zambuco was annoying, abrasive, and irritating. She thought Jane could do better. And she had been very vocal about her dislike of the man. No wonder Jane hadn't confided their relationship to her. Claire's heart twisted. Some friend she was. Her own best friend couldn't even confide in her because she was so closed minded.

But now, seeing how upset Zambuco was and the fact that he'd risk his job to come and ask their help ... well ... it made her wonder if she'd misjudged him. If he cared for Jane this much, then he couldn't be all bad. And Jane had seemed happier lately. Zambuco had, too. Jane must be having a positive effect on him, as he'd been less annoying. He'd even been dressing better. Perhaps it was time to bury the hatchet and make peace with the romance blossoming between Zambuco and Jane.

Claire glanced at Dom, who nodded his head ever so slightly.

"Will you help me? Please?" Zambuco pleaded.

"Okay, we'll get you that suspect, and it won't be Jane. But we need access to what the police know. We've been running this blind so far."

Zambuco slowly let out a breath. "Thanks. I brought the folders on the case. Let me get them from my car."

Chapter 17

"Let's move to the dining room." Dom thrust his chin in that direction as he rose from his chair. "We'll have more room to spread out on the table there."

Dom removed three of the place settings and stacked them on the sideboard, arranging the edges so they lined up perfectly.

From his perch in the cage, Romeo watched him with bright eyes. "Twchiller!"

"Yes, my friend, we're going to catch the killer." Dom hadn't been surprised to find out that there was something going on with Zambuco and Jane. He didn't really care much either way, although he wondered if Zambuco would eventually become part of their breakfast group. He wasn't too sure he liked that idea, but he couldn't complain that Zambuco's relationship with Jane was the impetus in him wanting to share police information with them.

A sharp knock on the door stole his attention, and he motioned Zambuco in. The detective fumbled noisily with the door latch. Then the door sprang open, and he lurched inside and made his way over to the dining table, where Claire was already seated.

"I'll make coffee." Dom got busy in the kitchen, glancing out into the dining room, where he could see Zambuco lining up manila folders on the table.

"Twarrogent!" Romeo tweeted.

Zambuco's head snapped up to the cage, his eyes narrowed. "Did that bird just say 'arrogant'?"

Claire snorted, using her napkin to cover her mouth, and pretend it was a sneeze.

"Oh no, he's just tweeting. Sometimes his tweets sound like words, but they're really not." Dom put three coffee mugs, sugar, and cream on the table then went back into the kitchen to retrieve a crystal dish with five cannolis placed symmetrically in a circle in the middle.

They busied themselves with fixing their coffees. Dom and Zambuco each took a cannoli. Claire passed. Apparently the cannoli wasn't part of her health regimen, Dom thought. Well, that was her bad fortune to miss out on the creamy, sweet pastry.

"Let's start with Elbert Daniels." Claire broke the ice since Dom and Zambuco were busy chewing.

"I've been working off the assumption that the two murders are connected. It's too much of a coincidence for them not to be," Zambuco said.

"Agreed," Dom mumbled around a mouthful of cannoli.

Zambuco took another bite, crunching into the middle of the pastry shell. Crumbs dropped onto his tie. He didn't bother to wipe them off, and Dom resisted the urge to brush them away. Zambuco swallowed loudly and said, "You go first. What have you found out about the murder?"

Claire and Dom shared what they knew about Elbert Daniels—the treasure-hunting club, the silent partner, the brooch Mari had had. None of this was news to Zambuco.

"Only someone who knew about that treasure chest could have put Elbert in there," Dom said.

"So it stands to reason that it was one of the other treasure hunters," Claire added.

"Obviously, but what was the motive?" Zambuco asked.

"That's what we can't quite figure out. At first we thought it was greed. Something to have to do with the treasure, but none of them seems to have gotten rich back then. If they found the treasure and split it four ways anyway, why not share with Elbert too? Why kill just him? It doesn't make sense."

172

"What if the motive wasn't money?" Claire asked.

Zambuco turned to her. "What are you thinking about? Jealousy? A lovers' quarrel?"

"Most people share secrets with their spouses. He probably told his widow about the treasure. Maybe they didn't have a good marriage, and she didn't want to share his portion ..." Claire let her voice drift off.

Zambuco's eyes narrowed. "No one mentioned any kind of dirty secrets or problems at home."

"But were you asking?" Claire paused for a few beats while Zambuco thought it over. "We weren't specifically asking about that either. Maybe we should have been."

"If you're right, and the widow did it, then the two murders can't possibly be connected. She moved away from the island shortly after Elbert went missing and died earlier this year."

Dom's eyebrow twitched. "She recently died?"

Could her death be connected or just coincidence?

Zambuco slurped his coffee. "It's a good theory, but it doesn't seem likely. Physically, it would be difficult for a woman to kill a man, stuff him in a treasure chest, and then bury it again. She would've had to have help."

"Maybe Elbert's wife was having a fling with one of the other treasure hunters and they were in on it together," Claire suggested.

"Ahh, killing two birds with one stone, so to speak," Dom said.

"Tweet!" Romeo tweeted his objection to the phrase loudly.

"Right, get rid of the husband, hook up with the wife, and get a double share of the bounty," Zambuco said. "So we're back to our original suspects, the members of the treasure-hunting club. I don't recall hearing about any of them having a relationship with Elbert's wife, but they might have kept it hidden."

"But if that was the motive, then why kill Mari Wilkinson now?" Claire asked.

"Maybe she knew something. Had an incriminating picture of Liz Daniels and the killer." Dom tapped his finger on his lips. "She did mention pictures when we were there, but we didn't see anything with the treasure hunters being friendly with a woman."

Claire glanced over at Zambuco. "Did you find any incriminating photos in there when you catalogued the crime scene?"

"No. None from that far back."

"Maybe we should go and look." Dom didn't dare say that he already knew where all the old photos were. Even with this supposed newfound alliance with Zambuco, he didn't want to let on that Robby had let them into the house.

"We could." Zambuco hesitated. "But I'm not sure that would be a good use of time. Most likely her old pictures were more benign. I doubt she had something that showed an overt affair."

Claire half stood, cocking her head sideways to look at the labels on the folders. She picked one and slid it in front of her then opened it up.

"Let's attack this from another angle. What do we have on the search and rescue for Elbert? Killers will often insinuate themselves into the investigation. Was Elbert's widow a part of it?" Claire asked. "If there are pictures, maybe I can read her body language in conjunction with the other searchers."

Zambuco gestured toward a folder. "Of course. She was front and center. In fact, almost the entire town trekked all over the island trying to find him. Even Mari Wilkinson was out there!"

They leafed through the folder, which was a compilation of police reports, newspaper clippings, and old pictures.

"This tells us nothing," Claire said. "I don't see any secretive couples here."

"Let's not be too hasty," Dom said. "You said most of the island was out on the search? Were the treasure hunters there? Maybe the killer was one of them, after all. We just said that killers like to insinuate themselves into the investigation."

"Or stay away altogether. Maybe one of them was conspicuously absent," Claire suggested.

Dom perched his half-moon glasses on his nose and reviewed the newspaper clippings. After a few minutes, he let out a breath. "Charlie Kuhn isn't here."

"Yeah, I know. I already checked," Zambuco said softly.

"Benjamin Hill and Quentin Crane are here," Dom said. "But not Bill Wilkinson."

"But he couldn't have killed Mari Wilkinson, so there's no connection if he was Elbert's killer," Claire pointed out.

"Maybe there is no connection." Zambuco ran a hand through his thinning hair. "It's unlikely someone from Elbert's time would physically be able to kill Mari. And the two living suspects, Hill and Crane, are old men. Crane is in a nursing home, for God's sake!"

"Don't underestimate the power of old men," Claire warned. "Mari was no spring chicken, and she was tiny and frail. She would have been easy enough to overpower."

"Even easier if you had a younger pair of arms to do the killing for you," Dom suggested.

"What are you thinking?" Zambuco asked.

"Allen Hill. He goes everywhere with Ben," Dom said.

"Ben did protest the digging very loudly. He was our first suspect." Dom turned to Claire, who nodded.

"Yeah, mine too," Zambuco said.

"Do you think Allen would be willing to commit murder to protect his grandfather?" Dom asked.

"Do you remember how protective he was of Ben while we were there? And Ben obviously lied to us about the treasure being found. We know that Charlie Kuhn took the treasure, whatever it was, to a collector on the mainland," Claire said.

"And if he lied about the treasure, maybe he lied about how he came into his money," Dom suggested.

"Or maybe he was able to make his initial investments because of the treasure," Claire said.

"And if Allen suspects this, he wouldn't want anything to come to light that might cause him to lose the family money," Dom said.

"Can we connect Allen to Mari's murder in any way?" Zambuco asked.

Dom slid another folder in front of him, the one on the Mari Wilkinson case. He opened it and quickly perused the notes, looking for eyewitness accounts of who had been near Mari's that day. "The neighbors only saw him with his grandfather, and that was a day or two before she was killed. Does he have an alibi for the night of the murder?"

"I did speak with them because they were seen there, and Allen and Ben are each other's alibis," Zambuco said.

Claire snorted. "He's tall. He might have wielded the murder weapon."

"Which we still don't have," Dom said. "Perhaps a search of the Hill mansion is in order."

Zambuco shook his head. "We need more evidence than that in order to get a warrant to search the premises."

They fell silent as Dom read over the rest of the evidence from Mari Wilkinson's case. "No sign of forced entry. Mari knew her attacker."

"That doesn't mean anything. No one locks their doors around here," Claire said.

"You're right. The killer could have walked right in. All we know is that they knew about the brooch and took it."

"Brooch?" Zambuco asked.

Dom glanced up over the rims of his half eyeglasses. "Yes. Don't tell me you didn't know. Mari had a brooch that Bill said came from the treasure chest."

"I knew the killer rifled through her jewelry, but I didn't know why. So they were looking for this brooch? Is it valuable?" Zambuco asked.

"Mari said it came from the treasure chest." Dom put the paper back in the pile, picked the whole pile up, and tapped the edge on the table so the papers were perfectly aligned before placing them back in the folder. "She didn't seem to think it had value, but I guess the killer figured it was proof of what was in the chest. Maybe they thought it could tie them to Elbert's murder somehow, or maybe it really was valuable and only the killer knew that."

"Well, if that's true, the killer can't be Charlie Kuhn." Claire's voice was tinged with relief. "If we're going on the assumption that Elbert's killer is the same person who killed Mari, that rules Charlie out for both killings."

"True, but if we go on the assumption that another, much younger person killed Mari so as to cover up for Elbert's killer, then Charlie is still in the running ... and I'm afraid that implicates Jane," Dom said.

"But we know it wasn't Jane, and that brooch ... if it was valuable..." Zambuco's face turned thoughtful. "We may have been coming at this from the wrong angle. And there is one thing you guys haven't addressed."

179

Dom stiffened in his chair, somewhat taken aback. "Oh? What might that be?"

Zambuco pushed up from the table and paced the small room. "If Mari's and Elbert's murders are related, then the killer must either be incapacitated or not know where Elbert was buried. Everyone knew about the pharmacy groundbreaking well in advance. It was approved six months ago, so why didn't he or she sneak over and dig up the trunk themselves before the groundbreaking? They could have avoided the discovery of Elbert's body in the first place, and things would have gone on as they have for the past sixty years. Maybe Mari's murder has nothing to do with covering up Elbert's."

"Twimpessed." Romeo clung to the side of his cage, giving Zambuco an approving look.

Dom was kind of impressed, too. Maybe Zambuco was a better detective than he had given him credit for. Dom slid his eyes over to Claire. She looked just as embarrassed as he felt. Zambuco had a darn good point. They'd been so focused on finding a motive that tied into the treasure and desperately trying to prove Jane or her father had nothing to do with it that they'd overlooked the obvious.

"Well, Ben did protest very heavily, and, if our theory about Allen killing Mari to cover for Ben is true, maybe he didn't know anything about Ben's involvement with Elbert until after the body was dug up," Claire said weakly.

Zambuco, who had paced over to the French doors and was looking out, spun on his heel to face them. "But Ben must have known his protests wouldn't stop the digging. Why not just remove the chest before the dig started? Why draw attention to the fact that he didn't want that area dug up? That would guarantee putting his name at the top of the suspect list, and Benjamin Hill doesn't seem that stupid."

Dom carefully brushed the crumbs from the table. What if they had assumed wrongly all along? What if they'd misconstrued the evidence? That would explain why most of it led them down the wrong trail. But given the absence of the brooch and the condition of Mari's room, it did seem like her murder had something to do with the brooch ...

"So you're saying Mari's murder may have been about the brooch, just not in the way we thought?" Dom said. "That certainly does shed some light on things that didn't quite make sense to me."

"What do you mean?" Claire asked.

"Do you remember Diane Randall, that nurse from Greenbriar Manor? On our first visit, I overheard her complain about needing money. We know she visited Mari Wilkinson, and Quentin had been telling her treasure-hunting stories. Maybe she somehow figured out Mari had that brooch and thought she could get away with stealing and selling it."

Claire snapped her fingers. "That's right! Alice saw the van driven by a woman matching her description at Mari's house ... and whoever cleaned out Elbert's storage locker matches that description, too."

"Storage locker?" A look of confusion crossed Zambuco's face, and Dom felt a perverse pleasure in knowing they had dug up another clue that Zambuco didn't know about.

"Elbert had a storage locker. Velma and Hazel told us he kept the equipment from the treasure-hunting club there, but when we went to take a look, someone had emptied it out," Dom said.

Zambuco looked at them incredulously. "But Elbert was dead. Who was paying for the locker?"

"Oh, Marcy just kept it for him. Old island policy that we take care of our own," Claire said. "Sure, if she needed to rent it, she would have, but she never needed that locker all these years. Her daddy thought maybe someone would come for the stuff eventually."

Zambuco shook his head. Mainlanders often didn't understand the tight-knit ways of the islanders. "Okay, but what does this have to do with this Randall woman? How does the storage locker relate to the brooch?"

"I'm not sure. But we found pebbles that could be from Greenbriar in the empty storage locker. Maybe Quentin told her they had stuff stored in there, and she thought she could cash in on some treasure," Dom said.

"And you know for sure it was this Randall woman that looked in the locker?" Zambuco asked.

Claire shook her head. "We aren't sure who cleaned it out, but Marcy told us someone was there before us to look at it, and the woman matched Diane Randall's description."

"That's just a guess. We need to know for sure if we're going to pursue this," Zambuco said.

"Easy enough to do," Dom said. "We'll just show a picture of Diane Randall to Marcy."

"How can we get a picture of her?" Claire asked.

"She's an employee of Greenbriar Manor. They have pictures for their records and employee badges." Dom turned to Zambuco. "And I'm sure Detective Zambuco here with his police credentials can get them to text a picture to his cell phone, which we can then show Marcy."

Zambuco already had his phone out, fumbling on the display screen with his thick thumbs.

"I can't believe we didn't think of this before. But it makes perfect sense. Elbert's killer isn't running amuck hiding evidence, and he didn't kill Mari. Her death had nothing to do with Elbert's, which is why no one dug up the treasure chest to keep it from being unearthed in the pharmacy groundbreaking. His killer is probably long dead. We've been barking up the wrong tree all along," Claire said.

"Twee!" Romeo tweeted.

"This could be our chance to get you that suspect your boss wants and clear Jane." Dom pushed up from the table and collected the dirty dishes.

Zambuco hung up the phone then stared at the display. "Robby's having them send a picture, and he's doing a background check on her to see if she has any priors."

Ping!

"That's it! That's the picture." Zambuco held the phone up, showing a picture of Diane Randall.

"That's her. The woman from Greenbriar," Claire confirmed.

"Well, what are we waiting for?" Zambuco started toward the door. "Let's go find out if she's our killer."

Chapter 18

Claire didn't waste time going to the storage unit office; the odds were Marcy wouldn't be there. "Let's go straight to the house. Hopefully she is home."

Zambuco pulled around back, and Claire was relieved to see Marcy's Prius in the driveway.

Claire hopped out of the car and sprinted to the house, pounding on the door. "Marcy, open up! We need your help."

A few seconds later, they heard the clank of the safety chain, the door cracked, and Marcy peered out at them. "Claire? What are you doing here?"

She opened the door the rest of the way, her eyes widening when she saw Zambuco and Dom. "What's this about? Has there been some trouble?"

"No, not really. We're looking into Mari's murder, and we think you might be able to help us," Claire said.

"Help you?" Marcy looked pleased at the thought. "Well, I'll do whatever I can."

"Remember when you told us a young woman came to look in Elbert's locker?" Dom asked.

"Yes, but I didn't get her name."

"That's okay." Zambuco held up the phone. "Is this her?"

Marcy took the phone then nodded. "Yes. Yes, I'm sure that is her." Her eyes flicked from Dom to Claire to Zambuco. "Oh my gosh, is she the killer?"

"Well, we don't know that for sure, but she has come up in the investigation, and we think she might be the person who broke in and stole everything out of Elbert's locker," Dom said.

Marcy frowned. "Broke in? Nobody broke in."

"But you said the locker was full two weeks ago, and when we looked in it, it was empty," Dom said.

Marcy nodded. "That's true. But nobody broke in. Remember, the lock was still intact, and it was the original lock. We had a hard time opening it. If someone broke in, the lock would have been cut."

"So whoever removed the items from the locker had a key?" Claire's stomach swooped. Was the theory about Diane wrong? How would she get a key to Elbert's locker? And if it wasn't her, then who emptied it?

Ding!

Zambuco grabbed his phone back from Marcy. "It's Robby. Dammit! Diane has no priors."

Claire's stomach fell even further. "This can't possibly be her first time doing something like this. It's too complicated. Could we have been wrong? Maybe she's just never been caug—"

Ding!

"It's Robby again." Zambuco scrolled his index finger on the display, and a smile slowly bloomed on his face. "I've been trying to teach the boy, and finally he's learning to take initiative, and it's paying off."

"What do you mean?" Dom looked at the phone over Zambuco's shoulder.

"Robby dug further into Diane Randall's background. It turns out Diane Randall is Elbert Daniels's granddaughter."

Dom sucked in a breath. "Of course! It all makes perfect sense."

"It does?" Claire asked.

"Yes. Consider the chronological order." Dom turned to Zambuco. "You said Elbert's widow recently died. That would be Diane's grandmother. And what happens when your grandparents die? You start to go through their things. Diane must've found something about the treasure in her grandmother's belongings."

Excitement shot through Claire like a double shot of caffeine. "She could have gotten the key to the storage unit. Maybe Elbert had had a journal like Charlie Kuhn or some kind of record of the storage location and what was in it. Maybe he'd even kept a record of the digs."

"So she would know exactly what kind of treasure they dug up," Zambuco said.

"Yes." Dom's face darkened. "She may have come for the treasure ... or she may have come for a more nefarious reason."

"What do you mean?" The ominous tone of Dom's voice sucked away Claire's excitement and set her nerves on edge.

"According to the file, the family never believed Elbert was lost at sea. They hounded the police to turn it into a homicide case. The police never did. This might have been impressed upon Diane at a young age. Maybe when her grandmother died, Diane found the evidence that enabled her to come back here and do more research into Elbert's death. Maybe she was just trying to find out what did happen back then ... and when his skeleton was dug up in the treasure chest, well, it might have been the catalyst that prompted her to set things straight for her grandfather."

"You mean, avenge his death?" Zambuco asked.

Dom nodded.

"Okay, but why kill Mari, then?" Claire asked.

"You, of all people, know that when people go off the rails, they aren't reasonable. She might have thought everyone in the treasure-hunting club had something to do with Elbert's death. Bill was dead, so she struck out against Mari to even things out," Dom said.

"She's new to Greenbriar Manor. Moved here a few months after the grandmother died. The timeline makes sense," Zambuco said.

"And Quentin has been telling her treasure stories," Claire said.

"Most likely prompted at her insistence," Dom added.

Zambuco's face hardened. He shoved his phone into his pocket. "And if she's coming here to get her revenge, then she's not going to stop at killing Mari."

Claire's heart skipped. "Oh my gosh, two other people involved are at Greenbriar. She could easily take her revenge on them, especially if she's in charge of their medications!"

"We have to stop her." Dom lurched off the steps and sprinted toward the car, and Claire and Zambuco followed.

"Poor, unsuspecting Quentin played right into her hands," Claire said.

Zambuco checked his watch as he jammed the car into gear. "The ferry leaves in five minutes. I'll call ahead and see if they can hold it until we get on. We must get to the mainland now ... before she claims her next victim!"

***

The ride to the mainland was a combination of grating nerves and frantic phone calls. Zambuco tried to place calls to the police station on the mainland as well as to Greenbriar, but his phone kept cutting out at the most inopportune moments. Claire spent most of the ride trying to urge the ferry driver to speed up, but he was already going as fast as he could.

When the ferry finally pulled into the dock, the three of them were already in the car, seat belts fastened and engine running. Since the captain had held the ferry for them, Zambuco's sedan was first in line, and he gunned it off the boat as soon as the crew lowered the ramp.

Zambuco broke some speeding laws, and they pulled in to Greenbriar in record time. The three of them burst out of the car and ran into the facility. Zambuco flashed his badge at the startled receptionist.

"Diane Randall. Where is she?" he snapped.

"Ummm... I don't—"

"She's in wing five giving the patients their meds," a nurse with a clipboard in her hand volunteered. "But I don't see wha—"

"That's where Lila's room is!" Claire took off like a shot, her heart pounding in her chest. She silently congratulated herself for sticking to her health regimen. She could easily run to Lila's room in record time. Dom and Zambuco were not as fit. She glanced over her shoulder to see them trailing behind as she skidded around the corner and down the hall to Lila's room.

Lila was sitting in her chair by the window, Jane seated across the small round table from her. Standing next to Lila was Diane Randall, the little paper cup they used to dispense medicine in her hand.

Claire rushed over and knocked the cup out of her hand. "No you don't!"

Diane's face registered surprise. "Just what do you think you're doing?" She scrambled to the floor to retrieve the pills.

Claire ignored her. Knowing that Zambuco would deal with Diane any second now, she crouched in front of Lila. "Mrs. Kuhn, are you okay?"

"Of course, dear. I'm feeling very chipper today, in fact."

"Claire, what is going on?" Jane looked at her as if she were crazy, then her attention flicked to the doorway, in which Zambuco and Dom had just appeared.

"I caught her in the act," Claire announced to Zambuco. "She was giving Mrs. Kuhn those pills."

Zambuco snapped white latex gloves onto his thick hands and took Diane's arm in one hand and the pills, which Diane had put back into the cup, in the other. "I'm going to need you to come with me."

Diane jerked her arm away. "What is the meaning of this?"

"You're wanted for questioning regarding the murder of Mari Wilkinson. I need to take you down to the station."

"Murder? I never murdered anyone! Let go of me!"

A crowd had gathered outside, and Claire saw Quentin Crane hovering just outside. Relief flooded through her. They'd made it in time before Diane could harm Lila or Quentin.

"I want a lawyer!" Diane yelled as Zambuco pulled her out of the room. "You can't just drag people down to the station without proof. I didn't do anything wrong!"

"We'll determine that down at the station. You can call your lawyer there," Zambuco said.

Something in the corner of the room caught Claire's eye. Jane's umbrella! She glanced out the window to see sunny blue skies. She whirled to face Jane, whose eyes were darting from Zambuco to Dom to Claire with a confused look.

"Frank, just what is going on here? Mom needs her medicine. Did Diane do something—"

"Jane," Claire interrupted. "Isn't that your umbrella? Why would you bring that today? It's not raining."

Jane looked even more confused. "I didn't bring it today. I left it here last week. But why—"

Claire interrupted her again. "So you didn't have it the night of the big downpour when Mari was murdered?"

"No. It was right here the whole time. I didn't have any umbrella, actually, and with it raining so hard we ... I mean ... I decided to stay in." Jane glanced uncertainly at Zambuco.

Claire walked over to the umbrella, bending over to inspect it but making sure not to touch it. The handle was in the shape of a white rose, thick and heavy. Could it be the murder weapon? It looked bulky enough, but Claire couldn't see any dried blood. Perhaps Diane had given it a good cleaning.

Claire slid her eyes back over to Diane. "No, I don't think the umbrella was here the whole time, was it, Diane? I think the umbrella made a little trip to Mooseamuck Island." Claire straightened and looked at Zambuco. "Detective, I believe I just found your murder weapon."

Dom's eyes narrowed, and he came to stand beside Claire. Claire wondered if he was a little jealous. It was usually his job to find the physical evidence. He bent closer then patted his eyebrow and straightened. "The handle looks sturdy enough. This needs to be tested for traces of blood."

A murmur drifted over the crowd. Zambuco let go of Diane long enough to grab the umbrella.

"What lovely flowers." Lila reached out toward the umbrella.

"These are not for you. I must take these with me, but I'll bring you prettier flowers later," Zambuco said softly to her.

"What exactly is going on?" Jane demanded.

"Alice James saw you at Mari's house the night she was murdered. Except it wasn't you, it was your umbrella." Claire pointed to the umbrella. "She said you were there right around the time of death. She also saw the Greenbriar shuttle there earlier that day, and a woman matching Diane's description was driving."

195

"The shuttle goes to the island quite often," Jane said.

Dom picked up where Claire left off. "What we think happened is Diane took the umbrella, either to implicate Jane or maybe just because it was raining. She drove over in the ferry and visited Mari. She discovered that she had some of the treasure and then came back later with the umbrella to kill her, using the umbrella as the murder weapon."

"What? I did not! I never took that umbrella anywhere!" Diane protested.

Dom raised a brow at her. "You didn't go to visit Mari Wilkinson that day?"

"No ... I mean yes. I did go to visit her, but I didn't kill her." Diane turned pleading eyes on Zambuco. "My grandfather was Elbert Daniels, and I've been trying to talk to all the people that knew him and find out more about him. That's all. I didn't kill anyone."

Claire snorted. Diane was good. She'd almost be convinced if she hadn't heard hundreds of other killers claim their innocence as well. "Well, if you truly are innocent, then you have nothing to fear. The law will prove it."

"You're Elbert's granddaughter?" Lila's eyes were sharp as she assessed Diane. "He was a lovely man. But you know, he never did go missing on that boat. That's what everyone thinks, but I'm not so sure. Charlie warned me not to talk about it, but I saw it. Elbert couldn't have taken his boat out because I saw-"

Claire's stomach flipped. Was Lila about to confess that she'd seen Charlie with Elbert's boat? Someone had to have set it adrift ... had that someone been Charlie Kuhn? Claire couldn't let Jane find out like this.

"Now, now, Lila, you've had a very upsetting afternoon. Maybe you should rest," Claire said, cutting off whatever the woman was about to blurt out as her eyes met Zambuco's. Apparently they were on the same wavelength. He gave her a curt nod then tugged Diane toward the door.

"Okay, okay. Break it up. Go back to your rooms. The party's over." Zambuco pulled Diane out the door.

Jane put a protective arm around Lila. "Was she really going to hurt Mom?"

Claire edged toward the door. They'd come with Zambuco, and, even though he had a prisoner now, he was their ride. "We're not sure. But your mom is safe now. I'll explain everything later."

Claire and Dom caught up with Zambuco in the lobby, where he was handing a still-protesting

Diane off to one of the officers that had responded to his earlier interrupted call.

"Well, that ties things up nicely." Zambuco rubbed his palms together.

"Maybe, but there's still one loose end," Claire said.

"Oh?"

"Diane couldn't have killed Elbert," Claire said.

"Oh, right." Zambuco made a face. "And that still might have something to do with Jane's father."

"Lila was about to say something earlier about Elbert's boat. I wonder if she really does know something or if it's just the dementia," Dom said.

"I didn't want her to blurt out something that might incriminate Charlie. I mean, we know he knew about the treasure because we have his journal, but I think we need some time to think things through and figure out what really happened to Elbert."

"We may never find out what happened," Dom said. "The people who know might be dead by now."

"We owe it to Jane to try, and now that the immediate danger is safely behind bars, we've got some time." Claire glanced out the window to where they were putting Diane in the back of the police car.

"And if Charlie was involved, we need to soften the blow as much as possible for Jane," Zambuco said.

"Agreed," Claire said then added, "Hopefully we won't have to give her the worst possible news."

Chapter 19

"I knew the two of you would figure out who the killer was." Mae beamed at Dom and Claire from across their usual table at Chowders, where they were all just finishing up their breakfast.

Dom's chest swelled with cautious pride. "Well, we still didn't figure out who killed Elbert."

"Pffft." Norma tapped the handle of her cane on the table. "You two found the important killer. The one that was running around the island now. Who cares who killed someone sixty years ago?"

"We did have some help from Zambuco, you know." Dom wanted to give credit where credit was due.

Norma snorted.

"I'm just glad the killer was caught." Alice's needles clacked together as she turned to Jane without dropping a stitch. "I'm sorry if I got you in trouble. I guess I just saw the umbrella and assumed it was you."

"That's why one should never assume," Claire said.

Jane waved her hand dismissively. "It's no problem. I can see how you would make that mistake. I'm just glad everything worked out."

"Odd, though, that Randall girl coming here after all these years to avenge the death of a grandfather she never knew." Tom stroked his chin. "Seems unlikely, doesn't it?"

Dom's left eyebrow jerked in an annoying twitch. It did seem unlikely, but all the clues pointed to her. Could they have been wrong? If that were the case, surely Zambuco would have called to let them know by now. He'd had Diane in custody since last night. Dom glanced at his phone, which sat on top of the table next to the plate that held his half piece of ricotta pie. No message.

"I'm just glad the island is safe again." Alice stuffed her skein of yarn and knitting needles into her large tote bag, threw some money on the table, and stood. "It was a little unnerving having a murder occur right across the street."

"Are you going over to the market?" Mae glanced at Tom. "We could go over with you. We have some feed for the goats to pick up."

As the three of them left, Jane pushed up from the table. "I have to get home and check on my kitchen. Shane is installing the cabinets today, and I want to see what they look like before I head over to Greenbriar to visit Mom."

Dom's chest tightened. Jane's words reminded him that he and Claire would have to spend the day digging into Charlie Kuhn's involvement in Elbert's murder and possibly bring bad news to Jane and Lila.

Next to him, the metallic sound of Norma digging pennies from her coin purse and stacking them on the bill caught his attention. Her gnarled, paint-stained hands painstakingly counted out the exact amount then grabbed the handle of her cane as she struggled out of her seat. "I've got some painting to do. Nice work on the capture, guys."

They watched Norma leave, then Claire said, "Well, I suppose we should get to work. We can't put off the inevitable, and the sooner we find out what Charlie was really up to and tell Jane, the better."

"Agreed. Seems like she has no idea—"

Ping!

The sound drew both their eyes to Dom's phone, where there was a brief text from Zambuco:

Umbrella Not Murder Weapon.

Dom looked up from the phone into Claire's troubled eyes.

"She must have used something else," Claire suggested.

"Of course ... but where is it?"

"Maybe she put it in the storage un—" Claire stopped midsentence, her eyes zoning in on the door. Dom turned to see Benjamin Hill making a beeline for their table with Allen fluttering behind him.

"What about over there, Grandpa? That table is near the heater." Allen pointed to a table on the other side of the room.

Ben scowled at him. "No, Allen. It's June and warm out. Besides, I have something to say to Dom and Claire. It's time we tell the truth about the past."

Allen's face paled. "But Grandpa, they're busy eating, and we should—"

Ben turned stiffly to face his grandson. "Let me talk, boy, or you can go wait in the car."

Allen lapsed into silence, but the downturn on his lips and the way he shuffled his feet told Dom he was not happy.

Ben turned to Dom and Claire. "Something's been eating away at me since we talked, and I have to come clean."

Dom raised a brow but waited patiently for the confession.

"I lied to you two when I told you we never found any treasure."

"Now is as good a time as any to tell the truth," Claire coaxed.

"Sixty years ago, we found that treasure chest, all four of us. But it wasn't what we expected."

"It wasn't?" Dom asked.

Ben shook his head. "We expected gold coins, like you see in the movies. But the chest was more of a shrine. Old letters tied with ribbon, a portrait of a young, pretty thing, an old journal, some jewelry but not enough to fill the chest. It was like we'd dug up someone's grave. We were disappointed. But jewelry's easy enough to sell, and we decided we might find some kind of history collector interested in the letters or journal. Bill took a piece to bring to the silent partner so he could take it to a collector and determine its value."

"And who was this silent partner?" Dom asked, wondering if Ben knew that it was Charlie.

"Hell if I know. Billy Wilkinson brought him in, and Billy was the only one to have contact with him."

"Okay, so what happened? Did they take it to the collector?"

"Not right away. You see, Elbert got a bunch of highfalutin ideas about historical value and whatnot. He didn't want to sell. Wanted to put it all in a museum instead."

Dom's brow resumed its annoying tingling. "Oh, really?"

"Yep. We had a big argument about it. You see, we'd invested a lot in equipment and borrowed from the investor. Some members felt they wanted to recoup that from the find. In the end we decided to find out how much it was worth before we made a decision."

"And was it worth a lot?"

"Nope. But turns out it wasn't worth being in a museum either. So we split the money—it was only a couple hundred each—and that was that."

"So the silent partner took it to the collector, who purchased the items, then Billy brought you each an equal share?" Claire asked.

Ben squinted and looked up at the ceiling. "No, that wasn't how it went. Billy got the name of the collector from the silent partner. But the silent partner didn't go with him. I think he was on a trip or something. Anyway, Elbert and Quentin took the treasure to the collector and came back with the money."

"Elbert and Quentin? What about Billy?" Claire asked.

"Billy got sick with the flu, and I had a work emergency at the last minute, so I couldn't go. Back then I was still building my investments and had to act quick with market fluctuations," Ben said.

"They took the trunk and contents?" The trunk was quite large, and Dom wondered how they would have gotten it to the mainland.

"Oh, no. Not the trunk. It was too big, and we didn't think it was worth much. They took the contents and stored the trunk in the storage unit ... or so I thought," Ben said. "Then we filled in the hole so no one else would dig there. Didn't know if there would be more treasure. We always planned on going back, but after Elbert disappeared, we didn't have the heart, especially since the first treasure wasn't worth much."

Dom was skeptical. It did seem like Ben was telling the truth, and it would be odd for him to admit all this now if he had something to hide, but his behavior at the dig had been curious. "If you thought the trunk was in the storage unit and had no idea Elbert was buried at the pharmacy dig site, then why did you protest the dig so vehemently?"

Ben shook his head and looked at the floor. "I guess I still had illusions that there might be real treasure there. After Elbert disappeared, the treasure club kind of fell apart. We never did dig there again. Not to mention I really don't want an ugly square-box pharmacy to muck up the landscape."

"But why did you lie about the treasure in the first place?" Claire asked.

Ben's cheeks turned pink. "I know it was stupid now, but we made a pact not to tell anyone, and I guess I still wanted to honor that pact. Initially it was because we didn't want others digging around there, but also we were a little embarrassed that we dug up a big treasure chest that wasn't worth anything." He shrugged. "It just didn't seem important to tell anyone."

"So you each got an equal share ... but then how did Elbert end up inside the trunk?" Claire asked.

"Beats me. I always thought he had drowned in the storm, just like they said."

Allen made a strangled noise and shot Ben a surprised look. Ben turned to face him, his eyes growing wide. "You thought I killed him, boy?"

"I ... no, I mean, I ..." Allen stammered.

"You should have more faith in me than that. Of course I didn't kill him! Elbert was a good friend. His family was good people. Which is why it confounds me that his granddaughter killed Mari. She seemed like such a nice girl."

"You knew her?" Claire sounded shocked. "I thought Elbert's widow moved off the island shortly after his disappearance. How did you know his granddaughter?"

"They did move. The kids were young, and I never even knew he had a granddaughter until she came to visit me the other day. Said she was visiting Elbert's old friends. Wanted to learn about her grandpa. You see, her grandma had just died, and she'd found a lot of Elbert's things in her attic. She let on that the family never accepted that he drowned at sea. I think she might've been investigating, but I had no idea she came here to kill people. And to think she killed Mari that very night ... it could have been me she killed."

"That night?" Dom asked.

Ben's face turned serious. "Yes, she was at my house the night of the downpour. The night Mari was killed."

Claire's forehead creased. "What time did she visit you?"

"She came just before supper. We eat at six precisely. I have to keep regular eating hours or my digestion is off. Then she stayed until the night ferry."

"But the night ferry leaves at eight," Claire said.

Ben nodded. "That's right. She left around seven forty-five to catch it. Otherwise she'd be stuck on the island."

Dom pressed his finger to his tingling eyebrow. "But she wasn't stuck on the island ... which means she couldn't have killed Mari."

"Wait a minute." Claire pulled out her phone, scrolling through the pictures. "Did you say the silent partner couldn't go to the collector because he was out of town?"

"Yes. If I remember correctly, that's why Elbert and Quentin went. You see, Elbert didn't trust—"

Claire thrust her phone at Dom, interrupting Benjamin. "Look! Charlie couldn't have killed Elbert. This is one of the pictures I took of his journal. Look past the journal page, though, underneath it at the bottom of the box. It's a plane ticket to Germany dated the day before Elbert disappeared. Lila said Charlie was always on his trips, and this time she was right. He was out of the country when Elbert disappeared."

Ben looked at her with confusion. "Charlie? Charlie who? What are you talking about?"

"Never mind that," Claire said. "When did Elbert and Quentin give you the money?"

Benjamin pursed his lips. "Funny thing, it was actually the day Elbert went missing. Least I think it was, since we found his boat adrift the next morning."

"So you were one of the last people to see Elbert?" Dom asked.

"Me? Oh no. I didn't see him that day, only Quentin. Quentin gave me my share. Elbert was busy."

"So, then, Quentin was possibly the last one to see Elbert ..." Claire said slowly.

"And Quentin is quite wealthy," Dom added.

Claire's face took on a troubled look. "Quentin missed his doctor's appointment the day Mari was killed. When we were in the garden with Lila, I overheard the nurse say he was gone all evening ..."

"Quentin could have easily taken the umbrella from Lila's room. In fact, Lila said he picked a bouquet, though at the time I thought she was talking about something in the past. Then when Zambuco took the umbrella, she thought it was a bouquet of flowers," Dom said.

"We may have made a terrible mistake. Quentin had means, motive, and opportunity for both murders!" Claire shot up from the table. "He must have known Mari had some evidence ... maybe even something she didn't realize she had. It was no problem when everyone still thought Elbert had been lost at sea, but now that he's been dug up and there's an ongoing investigation, he would have to silence her."

"Not just her." Dom's stomach turned to lead. "At Greenbriar yesterday, Lila was about to blurt out the name of the person she saw at Elbert's boat the day he supposedly disappeared at sea. You stopped her, thinking she was going to name Charlie, but ..."

"... It couldn't have been Charlie since he was in Germany, and if that person was Quentin, then he'll try to silence Lila next."

Chapter 20

Dom's phone dinged just as they rushed into Greenbriar Manor. He whipped it out of his pocket and looked at the display. "It's Zambuco. Says Diane isn't the killer. She has an alibi."

Claire looked at him incredulously. "No kidding."

Dom's thumbs flew over the screen as they hurtled toward Lila's room. "I'll tell him to meet us here."

"Hurry!" Claire turned the corner and barreled into Jane.

"Claire! What the heck?" Jane's face was etched with worry.

"Is something wrong? Where's your mom?" Claire asked.

"I can't find her. She's not in her room or the sitting area. But why are you running down the hall?"

Claire and Dom exchanged a glance.

"What?" Jane demanded.

Claire took her friend by the shoulders. "Don't panic. We've reason to believe Quentin killed Elbert, and he might want to harm your mom."

"What? Why?" Jane sucked in a breath. "Oh, yesterday she said she saw someone by Elbert's boat that day ..."

"Right. We've no time to waste. Where else could she be?" Dom asked.

"Maybe in the meditation garden?"

Dom and Claire had already turned and were sprinting in that direction before the last word was out of Jane's mouth. But before they even got there, Claire could see Lila wasn't out there. The garden was empty.

"Now what?" Claire rushed down the hall, looking into the sitting room where they'd spoken to Quentin the other day, peering into the bathroom. No Lila was to be found.

Dom grabbed a nurse. "Excuse me. Have you seen Lila Kuhn or Quentin Crane?"

"No, I don't think I have ..."

"I saw them," an aide interrupted from inside the library room. "I was wheeling Lila to breakfast, and Quentin came up and took over. Said they were having breakfast together. 'Course that was a few hours ago."

Claire didn't need to ask where the cafeteria was; Jane had already taken off down the hall, presumably in that direction. They followed Jane through the interior maze of Greenbriar Manor only to find a disappointingly empty cafeteria.

Jane grabbed one of the workers by the arm. "Emmy, did you see my mom?"

"Yes, she was here with Mr. Crane, but—"

"Did you see where they went?" Jane pleaded.

Emmy made a face. "No. They did leave together, though. Mr. Crane was pushing her in the chair. It was sweet. And Mrs. Kuhn was remembering her husband, Charlie. She said she was going to meet him, that he was waiting. She must have been having one of her memory episodes."

Jane sighed heavily, panic dancing in her eyes. "Well, that doesn't help us ... what direction did they go?"

"Wait a minute." Claire shot her arm out to stop Jane from running off. Something niggled at her brain. Lila had mentioned something about Charlie waiting for her the other day. Something Quentin had told her ... what was it? Oh yes! Golden doors.

Claire flicked her eyes to the entrance. White doors. The side door was also white. "Do you have any gold doors here?"

The cafeteria worker looked at her like she was crazy. "Gold doors? No, we have a more sophisticated look going. All the doors are painted white or natural wood."

"I know where there's some gold doors." They spun around to see a man in blue scrubs mopping the floor.

"Where?" Dom asked.

"Down in storage. That's where they keep all the older furniture, and there's an old television armoire down there from the Oriental decor we used to have. It's got a lot of gold on it." He shrugged. "Is that what you're looking for?"

"How do we get down there?" Claire asked.

The man thrust his chin toward the hall. "Take the elevator to floor G."

In the elevator, Jane stabbed the button repeatedly. "Come on, come on."

Dom gently moved her finger away. "Jane, we can't go rushing in. We may need the element of surprise on our side, and if we startle him, your mom might get hurt. Maybe you should stay upstairs."

"What? No way." Jane's eyes darted from Dom to Claire. Then she took a deep breath. "Okay, fine. I'll be quiet and follow your lead."

The elevator stopped and the doors whooshed open. Dom held his index finger to his lips as they stared out at a cavernous, dimly lit room filled with hulking shadows of furniture, shelving, and boxes.

"I don't see Charlie in there." Lila's voice, laced with suspicion, drifted over to them from an unseen corner of the room.

Jane lurched toward the voice, but Claire grabbed her elbow and pulled her back.

"Not yet," she whispered in Jane's ear. "Let's sneak around the edges. That way we'll have a better chance of disarming him."

Jane nodded, and Dom indicated for Claire and Jane to go left while he went right. Claire knew he meant to surround Quentin or at least surprise him from different directions.

Claire kept Jane beside her as she skirted shelving and ducked behind bureaus. They came to the corner of the room, and Claire gestured for Jane to be quiet as she peered around the corner of a stack of boxes.

Thirty feet away, Quentin had Lila out of her wheelchair. The poor woman stood on shaky legs, her hand clutching the door of a gigantic red-and-gold armoire with a bamboo motif on the side.

"Let her go, Quentin." Dom's voice sounded from Claire's left.

Quentin spun around to face Dom, snapping his cane up as if to hold him at bay. Alarm shot through Claire as she noticed the large handle. It

216

was thick and looked heavy ... could that be the murder weapon?

"What are you doing here?" Quentin demanded.

"What are you doing to Lila? Let her go," Dom persisted.

From Claire's vantage point, she could see the change in Quentin's face. His beady eyes softened, and he relaxed.

"Hey, we were just reminiscing about old times," Quentin said. "We come down here because it gets boring sitting in the same old sitting rooms up there."

"You said Charlie was waiting." Lila poked her head into the armoire then pulled it back out and looked at Quentin. "I don't see him."

Claire's stomach churned. Just what had Quentin been planning to do to Lila? Was he going to stuff her into the armoire and leave her in there to die, or kill her first? Beat her with the cane like he'd done to Mari? Her body probably wouldn't be found for days down here.

"Put her back in the chair and step away," Dom said.

"What are you getting all riled up for?" Quentin gently helped Lila back into the chair then started inching away from Dom. Claire wondered if he was trying to make a getaway.

Well, not on her watch. She motioned for Jane to stay put as she circled around to head Quentin off should he try to run away.

"Well, if you're going to sit with Lila, I guess I'll go to my room." Quentin took a tentative step.

"Not so fast. You're not going to get away with this. We know what you're up to." Dom had been inching his way toward Quentin and Lila and was now merely a few feet away.

"What?" Quentin was still playing dumb. "Lila and I are old friends."

Dom held up his phone. "It's over, Quentin. Police are on their way. Come peacefully, with some dignity."

Quentin glanced over his shoulder. Probably scouting out which direction to head to make his getaway.

"What? I have no idea what you're talking about." Quentin pivoted and took a running step toward the back of the room. Luckily Claire had anticipated the exact direction he would head. She stepped out from her hiding spot behind a tall china cabinet and blocked his exit.

"Admit defeat, Quentin. You wouldn't have gotten away with this. This body wouldn't stay buried for sixty years like the last one," she said.

Jane burst out of her hiding spot and ran to Lila. "Mom! Are you okay?"

"Janey, how nice to see you. I'm fine, just fine. Why wouldn't I be? But Daddy's waiting." Lila cast a tentative glance at the armoire.

"No, Mom, he's not waiting." Jane crouched down to hug Lila then glared up at Quentin. "I'm afraid your friend Quentin wasn't telling the truth."

"That's right, Quentin, what exactly is the truth?" Dom asked. "Time to come clean, and maybe I'll be able to persuade Zambuco to go easy on you."

Quentin looked around. With his exits blocked, he must have realized he was caught. His shoulders sagged in defeat, and he suddenly looked very tired.

"I had to try to stop her. She could have ruined everything," he said.

Dom nodded. "We guessed as much. We have proof that you killed Elbert. We don't need Lila's testimony on that. Zambuco is on his way to bring you in. And we know Diane Randall didn't kill Mari Wilkinson. You did. But why?"

"Why do you think? She had proof that would make everything come out in the open."

"The brooch?"

"Yes, that damn brooch. The one I gave to Billy Wilkinson to give to the silent partner wasn't actually one of the brooches from the treasure chest. I switched them and kept the good stuff for myself. Truth was I almost forgot about that darn thing. Didn't realize Mari still had it. But then Diane Randall mentioned that Mari had showed it to her, and I knew I had to try to get it back.

"I figured if she started waving that brooch around, things might start to come out, and people might put two and two together. Especially if that blabbermouth Benjamin Hill saw it. He'd know it wasn't the real brooch, and then people would start asking questions."

"So you killed her? Why couldn't you have just broken in and taken the brooch?" Claire asked.

"I was going to! I just wanted to sneak into her room and look for the brooch. But she wouldn't give it up. She was stubborn. I didn't want to kill her, but she left me no choice ... turns out killing is easier the second time around."

A chill ran up Claire's spine as she glanced at Lila. And even easier the third, apparently.

"You took quite a risk all these years leaving Elbert buried there in that lot. Weren't you afraid someone would dig him up?" Dom said.

"At first I was. But I can be pretty persuasive, and it was easy to come up with reasons not to dig there again. No one but the treasure club was ever interested in that lot. As the years went by, I became more and more certain that no one ever would be," Quentin said.

"But then they bought it for the pharmacy. Why didn't you just go and dig the trunk up and move it before the groundbreaking?" Claire asked.

"Damn old age," Quentin snarled. "It's not that I couldn't have done it, physically. I'm pretty strong, you know. It's just that being here in this place, I'm not as connected to the happenings on the island. I had no idea they were even thinking about digging there."

"So you almost got away with murder," Claire said.

Quentin slid his eyes over to Lila. "Yes, and I might've gotten away with it, too, if Lila hadn't had one of her lucid moments yesterday. When she blurted out that she'd seen someone at Elbert's boat that day, I knew I had to silence her. A shame she'd blurt it out now after all these years, but I couldn't let her tell anyone … even in her muddled state, if anyone believed her … well, I couldn't take the chance."

"You were very brave, Quentin." Lila's eyes shone, and she turned to Dom. "Quentin tried to save Elbert. I saw him diving in Smugglers' Cove near Elbert's boat. You know we have a lovely view from that spot in our backyard, don't you?"

221

Dom glanced from Lila to Quentin. "Except you weren't diving to save Elbert, were you? You were swimming away from the boat. Lila thought she saw you diving, but you'd just set the boat adrift. You took it into the cove, jumped out, and swam ashore. Left the empty boat so it would look like Elbert had taken the boat out and fallen overboard."

"That's right. Smart, wasn't I? I walked home and got my car then drove back to the cove, pretending like I had just spotted the boat bobbing around out there. I told them I had gone down to the cove crabbing. No one ever goes to Smugglers' Cove, and there's no houses around, so I felt fairly certain there would be no witnesses. I'd forgotten the Kuhns had that one little spot in their yard with the view. What are the odds Lila would be out there looking at the cove at exactly that time? All these years I never knew she saw me."

"But if she saw you, why did she never report it?" Claire wandered.

Dom answered for him. "Well, it sounds like she didn't realize what she saw. She thought Quentin had jumped in to save Elbert. It would be easy to think that if she saw him swimming in the water, especially if he told the cops that he jumped in after he noticed Elbert's boat was drifting without Elbert in it."

"That's exactly what I did. But I couldn't take the chance of her bringing attention to that now. Back then no one suspected foul play. Well, no one except Elbert's widow. But if they started looking into that now in light of Elbert's obvious murder, it could go bad for me. What if someone studied the timeline and realized the only way I could've gotten to Smugglers' Cove at the time Lila saw me was by boat? Elbert's boat."

"Is that what you saw, Mom?" Jane asked. "Did you see Quentin diving the day Elbert disappeared?"

"Yes, Janey. I told Daddy when he called from Germany. I was down at the edge of the property, you know with that beautiful view of Smugglers' Cove, and I saw Elbert's boat, which was odd, because no one takes their boat in there. It's just too rocky. Quentin was swimming around it. At first I thought they were just diving for lobster or crab. It wasn't until later on that we found out Elbert was missing, and then I heard that Quentin had been diving in the water to try to save him. Such a nice man."

Claire and Dom exchanged a raised-brow look. Nice man, indeed.

"Sounds like the perfect cover-up. Acting like the hero as if you were diving to save Elbert. But why kill him and go to such an elaborate ruse, especially since the treasure was virtually worthless?" Claire asked.

Quentin barked out a laugh. "Virtually worthless? That's what they all thought. And Elbert had his highfalutin ideas of putting it all in a museum. He was talking crazy, and I couldn't let him persuade the others, especially since I'd already set it up so that they would think the treasure was worth a lot less than it actually was."

"And with it not being worth much, they could be persuaded to put it in the museum a lot easier, since they wouldn't be losing out on a lot of money to do so," Dom said.

"That's right. My plan almost backfired because of that." Quentin's face turned sour. "And to top it all off, Elbert didn't trust me and insisted on coming to see the collector. Well, I couldn't let that happen. I had to kill him. Then I took those letters to the collector myself. Those letters were from William Kidd's brother to his mistress, and they believed they were only worth thousands? Serves them right for being so dumb."

"Just what were they worth?" Claire asked.

"Hundreds of thousands."

"So you swindled your friends out of hundreds of thousands of dollars and then killed one of them?" Dom asked.

Quentin made a face. "Well, when you put it that way, it sounds so harsh. I was just doing what I needed to do to support my family and myself in my old age. I didn't have money like the others. And I was frugal with it, too, spending it just a little bit at a time so no one would notice and saving most of it so I could be comfortable in my old age."

"You almost got away with it, too—"

"Just what is going on down here?" A nurse in green scrubs stood staring at them, her gaze flicking from Lila to Dom to Claire to Quentin. Claire had been so engrossed in Quentin's confession that she hadn't even heard the nurse approaching. Those thick-rubber-soled shoes really muffled any footsteps.

Quentin must have seen the distraction as his chance to escape. He pivoted away from Claire and made a break for it, darting in between an old sofa and a baker's rack.

Claire bolted after him. He zigged. He zagged. But then he came to the wall and had to take a sharp right turn. As he pivoted, his knee twisted and gave out. He fell to the floor with a loud yelp.

"Mr. Crane!" The nurse ran over and crouched next to him. "Well, now you've done it. Your leg is not strong enough for that kind of activity. I told you that you shouldn't have missed your doctor's appointment the other day. Maybe next time you'll take heed of my words, and your leg will be strong enough for these kinds of shenanigans."

"I don't think there will be a next time." Zambuco walked up to the group, flashing his badge. "Quentin Crane, you're under arrest for the murders of Elbert Daniels and Mari Wilkinson."

Chapter 21

The next morning, Claire and Dom sat at their usual breakfast table in Chowders with Mae, Tom, Alice, Norma, Jane, and, much to Claire's dismay, Zambuco.

As she had feared, it appeared Zambuco might become a regular at their breakfasts. But looking across the table at the happy smile on Jane's flushed face, she couldn't be upset about it. If Zambuco brought Jane this much happiness, then Claire would have to give him another chance. Jane was a good person, and she clearly saw something in Zambuco—maybe he wasn't such a bad guy after all.

"I don't condone murder, but I have to hand it to Quentin. He spent that money judiciously over the years, and no one would've suspected he'd come into five hundred thousand dollars back then," Tom said.

"Yeah, he set himself up to spend his golden years in a nice place like Greenbriar," Mae said. "A lot of us won't be that lucky."

"Too bad he'll probably be spending it in the state penitentiary now," Zambuco said.

"I'm just glad my dad wasn't involved." Jane shot Claire a sheepish glance.

"So, you were lurking around trying to find out if your father was involved," Claire said.

Jane placed her hand on Claire's arm. "Yes, and I'm sorry I didn't fill you in, but when I saw that plaid shirt in the trunk, I immediately thought of my dad. He had a shirt just like that."

"Is that why you were at the storage unit that day? Digging up clues?" Dom asked.

"Yes. I was looking for pictures or anything to prove ... I don't know ... that my dad wasn't involved, I guess. I did find an old photo of him and Elbert, both with the same plaid shirt. Mom said there was a sale at E-Mart on the mainland that year, and they ended up with the same shirt." Jane took her hand back and dipped her toast in a puddle of egg yolk. "Funny how she can remember little details like that but not what she did yesterday."

"You found that box with his journal in the storage locker," Claire said.

Jane's eyes widened. "How did you know about that?"

Claire swallowed the pang of guilt that rose up in her throat. She felt bad for snooping in Jane's house but consoled herself with the fact that it was for Jane's own good. "Let's just say you're not the only one that avoided telling the truth in this case."

"But that box didn't prove anything. All that was in it was some cryptic journal, old plane tickets, and passports." Jane scooped some egg white onto her yolk-soaked toast. "But I did find another one of his baseball cards and just found out this morning that it's worth quite a bit of money."

"Baseball cards?" Dom said. "I remember you mentioned he had a collection before. Is that how you came into all this money?"

"Yes." Jane glanced from Dom to Claire. "Didn't I tell you? When Mom's memory started failing, I knew I'd probably have to put her in some kind of living arrangement. I figured we'd need the money from selling the house, so I started going through her vast accumulation, and I discovered some savings bonds that Dad had bought decades ago. They'd already come to maturity and were no longer earning interest, but I could still cash them in, and it turned out they were worth quite a bit. Along with them was a letter—the bill of sale from his baseball card collection that he sold at auction. He also had the trip he took to the mainland to show them to the collector documented in that box from the storage unit. How else did you think I could afford to put Mom in Greenbriar and buy a new car?"

"Well, I did wonder ..." Claire said. "That actually explains a lot. We thought your father took the trip to the collector with the treasure, but that wasn't it at all. That trip was to sell his baseball cards."

"I'm sorry if I forgot to mention it, Claire." Jane's cheeks turned crimson as she glanced sideways at Zambuco. "I've been rather distracted this past year."

Dom brushed crumbs from the pizzelle cookie he'd had as breakfast from his fingertips. "So, if you were investigating your father's involvement, then you must have figured out he was involved with the treasure-hunting club."

Jane grimaced. "I did, but I didn't know in what capacity. He wasn't in the club, according to Ben. But then Mari said something about a silent partner ... an investor, and I realized that was my dad."

"So, you did go visit Mari that day when Alice said she saw you?" Dom asked.

"No, not that day. I went the day before." Jane turned to Claire. "I didn't lie to you guys about that. I really wasn't there on the day you asked about, and I really did leave my umbrella at Greenbriar."

"And Quentin took it when he went to kill Mari." Mae's voice was unsteady.

Zambuco nodded. "Yes, and we did find blood on the handle of his cane, so the umbrella wasn't the murder weapon as we first suspected."

Norma rapped the table with her cane. "That's all well and good, but what I want to know is what's going to happen to all the money Quentin stole? Does he have to give it back?"

Zambuco patted his lips with the white paper napkin. "That's a legal muddle. First they have to prove they were owed the money. Other than Charlie's journal, which is only an inventory of the equipment, there were no records. No paperwork to even prove they had an agreement. Even the auction house where Quentin sold the letters can't provide records from that far back."

"That's right," Claire said. "I Googled it and found a mention of the letters in an old newspaper, but it didn't say who had owned them. It didn't even say where they were dug up!"

"At auction, the seller can remain completely anonymous," Norma said. "But we all know it was Quentin, and I think he should make restitution."

"I'm just glad it wasn't that nice Diane Randall," Jane said. "Poor thing just wanted to find out more about her grandfather and ends up being accused of murder!"

"So, it was her who cleaned out the storage unit, then?" Tom asked.

Zambuco nodded. "She found the key with a label on it in her grandmother's things. She said it was full of dirty old equipment."

Norma's eyes narrowed. "No treasure?"

"Nope."

"Harumph," Norma said. "Well, if she did find treasure, I guess she deserves it after what happened to her grandfather."

"That explains the red pebbles we found inside," Dom said to Claire. "She had them stuck in the treads of her shoes from Greenbriar."

"The whole time she was getting treasure-hunting stories from Quentin, she had no idea she was talking to her grandfather's killer," Alice said somberly.

"I wonder why he told her those stories. Seems like he would have rather kept mum about them," Mae said.

"Pride and boastfulness," Claire said. "He didn't know they were going to dig where he'd buried Elbert, and Diane never mentioned she was Elbert's granddaughter. She was keeping it close to the vest since she was also trying to figure out what really happened to him. Quentin thought he'd gotten away with murder, and his ego got the best of him."

"Then once he heard Elbert's body had been found, it was too late. He'd already been telling her about their treasure hunts, and it would seem suspicious if he suddenly stopped," Dom added.

"Well, I never did like Quentin anyway." Alice turned her attention to Zambuco. "So, will you be making breakfast with us a regular thing?"

Zambuco favored Jane with a sickly sweet smile that almost made Claire gag. Even worse, Jane was returning it.

"You know, I think I might," Zambuco said.

"Does that mean Claire and I will be able to consult on the next murder?" Dom asked.

Zambuco's smile faded. "You two did do a good job on this case, but consulting on future cases ... I wouldn't count on it."

The end.

COZYMYSTERY to 88202 (sorry, this only works for US cell phones!)

Want more of Claire and Dom's adventures? Buy the rest of the books in the series:

A Zen For Murder
A Crabby Killer

A Note From The Author

Thanks so much for reading, "*A Treacherous Treasure*". I hope you liked reading it as much as I loved writing it. If you did, and feel inclined to leave a review, I really would appreciate it.

This is book three of the Mooseamuck Island Cozy Mystery Series. I plan to write many more books featuring Dom and Claire. I have several other series that I write, too - you can find out more about them on my website http://www.leighanndobbs.com.

This book has been through many edits with several people and even some software programs, but since nothing is infallible (even the software programs), you might catch a spelling error or mistake and, if you do, I sure would appreciate it if you let me know - you can contact me at: lee@leighanndobbs.com.

Oh, and I love to connect with my readers, so please visit me on facebook at http://www.facebook.com/leighanndobbsbooks

Signup to get my newest releases at a discount: http://www.leighanndobbs.com/newsletter

About the Author

USA Today best selling Author, Leighann Dobbs, has had a passion for reading since she was old enough to hold a book, but she didn't put pen to paper until much later in life. After a twenty-year career as a software engineer with a few side trips into selling antiques and making jewelry, she realized you can't make a living reading books, so she tried her hand at writing them and discovered she had a passion for that, too! She lives in New Hampshire with her husband, Bruce, their trusty Chihuahua mix, Mojo, and beautiful rescue cat, Kitty.

Find out about her latest books and how to get discounts on them by signing up at:

http://www.leighanndobbs.com/newsletter

Connect with Leighann on Facebook
http://facebook.com/leighanndobbsbooks

More Books By Leighann Dobbs:

Mystic Notch
Cats & Magic Cozy Mystery Series
＊ ＊ ＊

Ghostly Paws
A Spirited Tail
A Mew To A Kill
Paws and Effect

Mooseamuck Island
Cozy Mystery Series
＊ ＊ ＊

A Zen For Murder
A Crabby Killer

Kate Diamond
Adventure/Suspense Series
＊ ＊ ＊

Hidden Agemda
Ancient Hiss Story

Blackmoore Sisters
Cozy Mystery Series
＊ ＊ ＊

Dead Wrong
Dead & Buried
Dead Tide
Buried Secrets
Deadly Intentions
A Grave Mistake
Spell Found

Lexy Baker
Cozy Mystery Series
* * *

Lexy Baker Cozy Mystery Series Boxed Set
Vol 1 (Books 1-4)

Or buy the books separately:

Killer Cupcakes (Book 1)
Dying For Danish (Book 2)
Murder, Money and Marzipan (Book 3)
3 Bodies and a Biscotti (Book 4)
Brownies, Bodies & Bad Guys (Book 5)
Bake, Battle & Roll (Book 6)
Wedded Blintz (Book 7)
Scones, Skulls & Scams (Book 8)
Ice Cream Murder (Book 9)
Mummified Meringues (Book 10)
Brutal Brulee (Book 11 - Novella)

Contemporary
Romance
* * *

*Sweet Escapes*
*Reluctant Romance*

84702892R00134

Made in the USA
Lexington, KY
24 March 2018